JQ

WITCH QUEEN

Joanna of Navarre's childhood was dominated by her cruel and scheming father, Charles of Navarre. He introduced her to the arts of healing and sorcery that were to brand her with the unwarranted reputation of witch. When widowed, Joanna becomes queen to Henry IV of England and is a good stepmother to all his sons, including Hal, the future Henry V. But her refusal to invest her fortune in Hal's war-raging in France brings on a dreadful vengeance.

Books by Maureen Peters
in the Linford Romance Library:

ENGLAND'S MISTRESS

MAUREEN PETERS

◆

WITCH QUEEN

Complete and Unabridged

LINFORD
Leicester

First published in Great Britain in 1990 by
Robert Hale Limited
London

First Linford Edition
published 1998
by arrangement with
Robert Hale Limited
London

British Library CIP Data

Peters, Maureen, *1935 –*
Witch Queen.—Large print ed.—
Linford romance library
1. Love stories
2. Large type books
I. Title
823.9'14 [F]

ISBN 0–7089–5315–8

Published by
F. A. Thorpe (Publishing) Ltd.
Anstey, Leicestershire

Set by Words & Graphics Ltd.
Anstey, Leicestershire
Printed and bound in Great Britain by
T. J. International Ltd., Padstow, Cornwall

This book is printed on acid-free paper

Prologue

1403

Perhaps, in the end, becoming Queen was worth all the rest of it. Long years of waiting, of planning for what had begun as no more than a passing fancy because she had been bored, were swept away in the February snowflakes that scudded across Westminster Courtyard.

The Abbey reared before her like some crouching beast, doors open to reveal the scarlet tongue of carpet within. She had walked there beneath a canopy of gold and crimson to protect her from the elements. The crowds, straining to catch a glimpse of their queen, had been granted no such protection. Joanna thought them crazy to stand in such weather, merely to look at a woman to whom they would never speak. There was a gulf between them and such as herself that she had not the faintest desire to breach. This did not mean that she wished them ill. Unlike her father, whom she remembered with a mixture of dread and love, Joanna had in her no vein of cruelty. Yet, all her life, she had been bound to fierce, warlike men, and not once had she been the first woman in their lives. No green youth had ever whispered words of love. Even Oliver de Clisson had been married when they met. Best not to think of De Clisson at this time. Best to pace steadily on, measuring her steps carefully so that the purple mantle would not drag at her shoulders. Lined in the same silver brocade as her tight-fitting gown there was about it a quality of the night. She was moon rather than sun, her pale hair ash-coloured, her eyes translucent hazel, her tall figure still willow-slender though she had borne eight children.

Within the Abbey colours blazed at her from trumpets, gowns, copes, banners and gilded armour. The King was watching the ceremony from an upper gallery. She flicked a brief, upward glance and saw him standing in the shadow of a tall screen.

'This day is your day,' he had told her. 'I want none of the glory.'

He had wanted to impress upon his Council that he held his bride of Navarre in the highest respect. She was aware there had been murmuring against this marriage, that many found it slightly shocking that Henry had taken another wife when the five sons and two daughters of his first marriage had secured the succession. And he had not chosen a young maiden, but a widow of thirty-three with a family of her own. Perhaps they expected him, at thirty-seven, to live like a monk for the rest of his life.

There were monks here in the Abbey. Too many of them, she thought sourly, aware of their bat-like flutterings against the brilliance. She had never cared for monks or nuns or for the panoply of

Christian ritual. Nevertheless it was necessary to endure them, to pay lip service to their beliefs.

'It is safer so,' her father had said. 'It is safer so, my child.'

He had spoken to her kindly on that occasion. At other times he had not spoken at all, but looked at her with silent contempt, once having found her weeping over a dead bird. She had been about five years old then and the bird had been her pet, but she had seen the expression in her father's eyes, and that look had dried up her tears as if it were a sponge. She would never weep again before him, she had resolved, and kept the vow. All her weeping was pressed down and held inside herself and there was nothing but a dull ache where tears should have been. It had made her very strong, she thought now, but also very lonely. At the most important moments of her life she had always been lonely.

1

'I have chosen a husband for you,' her father said.

He had summoned her to his chamber to give her the news. It was rarely that he spoke with her in private about ordinary matters. The times when they were alone together were reserved for the dark of the moon when he talked to her of the forbidden things. Now she stood before him, a tall child of nearly eleven, her fair hair braided, the bodice of her gown flat.

'Are you interested in his name?' Her father's voice sharpened. She had learned long ago to dread that note in it. Usually it was the prelude to one of his icy, silent rages that could only be mitigated by some act of cruelty.

'I was about to ask you, father,' she said hastily.

'It is John of Castille. He is not

5

yet twenty and handsome, so you have good reason to thank me.' The sharpness, to her relief, was gone. His voice now held nothing more alarming than a dry amusement.

'I have not met him,' she said.

'It is not necessary for you to meet him,' her father said. 'It is sufficient that his father and I consider him to be suitable. You are a princess of Navarre, Joanna, not a scullery maid.'

'Your choice will please me,' she said, even more hastily.

'The marriage will bring me a useful ally.' He spoke musingly, as if he had forgotten to dismiss her. 'I have more right to the throne of France than either Richard of England or Philip de Valois. Yet the Salic law debars me because my descent comes through the distaff line. So I play one against the other and acquire what allies I can muster. You understand, daughter?'

She understood little, save that she was a pawn in the game of kingdoms being played all over Europe. In the game the hopes and fears of a princess, whatever her age, meant precisely nothing.

'You understand?' he repeated. His eyes, of a darker hazel than her own, glowed as if somebody had lit a little red flame at the back of each pupil.

'Yes, father,' she said at once, adding, 'I shall be pleased to marry John of Castille.'

'I'm marrying your brother Charles to Castille's daughter,' her father said.

She gave a small, docile smile. Her older sister and her brothers were practically strangers to her. They were being reared in various castles and met together rarely on state occasions. Joanna was the only one of his children whom Charles of Navarre kept with him. She occasionaly wondered why, for it was certain that he didn't love her. Indeed there were times when he looked at her almost with hatred, and she tried, on those occasions, to become so small that she was almost invisible. There had been a mother once, but her she recalled so vaguely that it was like having a picture in her mind of a dream once dreamed.

'Navarre and Castille will be a formidable partnership,' her father said. He sounded pleased again. Joanna allowed herself a little sigh of relief. When Charles of Navarre was not pleased a thick cloud of dread hung over the castle and the servants trod softly, not knowing if their lord's eye might fall upon them, his thin lips curving as he planned whippings and brandings. His cruelty was a byword far beyond the realm he ruled. Charles the Bad they called him, and once a knight had had the temerity to say so to his face. The company had frozen, many beginning to recite prayers for the dying behind unmoving lips, but Charles had, to everybody's amazement, merely pulled at his little pointed beard and smiled, and no harm had come to the rash young man.

'That is all, daughter,' her father said at last. He held out his hand for her to kiss and she bent obediently. He had beautiful hands, thin and shapely and strong, the nails long and polished, each finger blazing with jewels. There were more jewels thickly clustered at the hem and high collar of his robe. Though it was summer he wore velvet and fur, and throughout the castle braziers glowed.

'If my father goes to hell as people say he will,' Joanna found herself thinking, 'then he will at least be warm.' She stifled an uncharacteristic giggle as she went out into the corridor. Navarre was a small kingdom but its castles were large. Joanna had spent her whole life in one or another of them and was accustomed to the high, thick walls and slit windows, built more to repel attack than to provide comfort for the dwellers within. Beyond the outer bailey the plains of Navarre, rust-red under the burning sun, stretched to the horizon.

There were parts of the castle where she never ventured. She knew there were dungeons where people who displeased her father were kept. Once, standing in a small courtyard near to a grating, she had heard a long drawn-out howl, more like an animal than a man, and caught a glimpse of a face, blood streaming from empty eye-sockets, before her nurse called her to come away. Ever after she had avoided that wing, confining herself to the hall and chapel and her own apartments, and taking care not to look out of her window on days when there was a hanging or flogging.

They were not always residing in the same place, Charles moving on every three or four months, but as their furniture was sent on ahead and all the castles were built on the same lines they ran together in her mind into one castle. She supposed, when she was married, she would live in the same way she had always lived, save that she would have no instructor in the forbidden arts.

That was one thing she shared with her father and nobody else, for he had impressed upon her early that the lessons she had with him were secret ones.

'Trust nobody with this knowledge. It will protect you from harm and enable you to vanquish your enemies with no chance of your being blamed,' he had instructed her. 'Such arts are passed from father to daughter, from daughter to son. I learned from my mother and some day you will teach them to your son.'

There were occasions, when she measured out henbane and wolfbane and crushed seeds of laburnum, that she wished he had chosen her elder sister as his pupil. It was amusing to pound and brew, but there were prayers to be said while one did the work. It was hard enough to memorise the ordinary prayers, but these had to be recited backwards, and the names were unfamiliar. All that she knew, even before her father cautioned her, was that such names were never under any circumstances to be repeated in church.

'We attend church because it is the custom and we may require the Pope on our side one day,' Charles had told her, 'but there is no need to take the mouthings of monks seriously. What is important, daughter, is knowledge, because knowledge brings power. When you have power you can rid yourself of all opposition.'

She had sighed inwardly at that because the truth was she would have preferred to use power to provide herself with a few friends. Few children of her own age ever visited the castle, and sometimes it was lonely to bear the weight of her father's teachings with nobody to play catchball or hoodman blind in the few hours of leisure she was given. Perhaps her husband would do so, she reflected, and wanted to giggle again.

A few weeks later she was summoned once more to attend her father. He had been absent from home, an event she always viewed with mixed feelings. Certainly she missed him as a dutiful child was obliged to do, but there was no denying that with his departure something cold and dark lifted from the castle. Usually, when he returned, she was the one appointed to hold the welcome cup, but he had ridden in at dawn while she still slept.

'And in a bad humour, my sweeting,' her dame had cautioned. 'I don't know what puts him out of humour, but you'd be wise to tread warily.'

It was unnecessary advice. When Charles of Navarre was in a bad humour, the whole world trod warily.

He was giving instructions to his steward when she entered the chamber, and she waited, bent prudently to her knee, until he had waved the man away and motioned her to rise.

'Castille has bedded Aragon and will have none of you,' was his greeting.

'Oh.' As she could think of nothing else to say, she said again, 'Oh.'

'Don't stand there like a dolt!' Charles said irritably. 'You've been thrown over, jilted, the House of

13

Navarre has been insulted.'

'I am sorry for it,' she said quickly.

'It is John of Castille who will be sorry for it,' Charles said. 'He had best say a prayer before he eats or drinks anything in future! It is your mother's family who seek to govern Spain too, by isolating me among my enemies. But they underestimate me, Joanna. I'll not sit tamely by while I'm cheated and betrayed.'

'Indeed not!' Joanna said fervently.

'Aragon and Castille have my kingdom in a vice, pressing upon my western and eastern borders, but you will elude their trap,' he told her. 'I'm sending you to my stronghold of Breteuil in Normandy. You'll be safe there.'

Safe from what, she wondered, but forbore to enquire. It was never wise to question father, even when he was in a good mood.

'You sail tomorrow,' Charles said. 'You'll land at Anray and cross the border into Normandy. When I've flung off the yokes of Aragon and Castille you will return.'

She had known that when she wed she would leave Navarre, but this was no marriage. This was flight and, for an instant, she wanted to protest that she was a princess and had no intention of running away. But the only time she had ever protested against her father's will he had hanged a litter of puppies and made her watch, so she bit down hard on her lower lip and remained silent.

'Remember what I have taught you,' he said, giving her a sharp look. 'Trust no man for all men are evil. Keep the secret knowledge inside your own head until the day comes when you need to use it and then use it swiftly, without mercy.'

'Yes father,' she said, and knelt again to kiss the cold ringed hand.

This was the first time in her life she had ever been at sea, and the immensity of the water measured against the ship in which she travelled disconcerted her.

She had not realised that anything could be quite so vast, so clear on the surface but so impenetrable beneath. Her father had not bidden her a second farewell but ridden out again, carrying with him the cold, dark cloud that hung all over the places where he was residing. Sometimes Joanna had had the fancy that if she put out her hand she would touch its icy, sharp edges. Though her dame moaned and began to declaim a prayer for safety on the perilous sea, Joanna, as they went up the gangplank, found her momentary hesitation swept away in a sudden rush of excitement. This was the first time she was actually going somewhere by herself and had she not been certain that her conduct would be reported back to Charles, she would have skipped along the deck.

The Bay of Biscay was ill-tempered even in the summer, it was said, but on this voyage the seas failed to live up to their reputation. Calmly smiling day followed calmly smiling day and at night the wind was no greater than that which would rock a child asleep. Even her dame consented to recover from the seasickness that had sent her groaning to her cabin and totter along the deck, her wimple pulled up to her nose lest the sea breezes set her back teeth aching.

It was almost a pity to see land ahead and a group of horsemen clustered on the jetty of the harbour.

'My lord father arranged for someone to meet us and escort us over the border.' Joanna shaded her eyes with her hand and looked across the dancing wavelets, but there was no face there which she recognised.

The gangplank had been lowered and she remembered her manners, thanking the Captain for a safe voyage and leaving money from her purse for the crew before she stepped on to the slats, sliding her hand along the rope, holding her head high as she had been trained.

'My Lady Joanna.' A tall gentleman

with eyes the same hazel as her own, bowed before her. 'Sir Oliver de Clisson, at your service.'

'Sir.' She gave him her hand shyly, aware of an amused glint in the hazel eyes that looked down into hers. He was one of the handsomest men she had ever seen, though he was already quite elderly — at least thirty, she reckoned — and found herself blushing for no reason.

'If you will come this way we have horses waiting.' He took her hand and led her along the jetty to where the others waited. She recognised none of them but when a fair-haired man, gold surcoat over the light armour he wore, stepped forward, she had the sudden queer sensation of being whirled back into a time she couldn't quite recall.

'We have not met since you were a babe,' the newcomer said. 'You have grown prettier since then, but you are not so pretty as your mother was.'

'You — knew her?' Joanna peered at him more closely.

'She was my sister. I am your uncle of Berry, child. Your uncle of Burgundy would have ridden to greet you too, but he had state affairs to settle.'

She had drawn back from his offered embrace, her whole body stiff with alarm. These were the uncles against whom her father had warned her many times. 'They support the De Valois claim to France though their own sister was married to me. I would gladly hang their heads over my gates if I could tempt them into Navarre.'

Shivering a little she said, 'I am b-bound for Normandy, my lord uncle. My father — '

'Your father will be less apt to plot against the throne of France if his children are being reared in Paris,' he interrupted genially. 'Your brothers are already there and enjoying a fine summer. You will enjoy Paris too. It's a lovely city.'

'But I am supposed to be going to Normandy,' she repeated helplessly.

'The plans are changed, niece.' His

smile was still genial but she sensed steel. 'Come, we've a palfrey schooled to a maiden's hands, and convent lodging for the night.'

It would have been useless and undignified to make a fuss. She went with him, holding back fear. Though she knew little of statecraft, she was fully aware that she was now a hostage for her father's behaviour and she wished she could be as sure as her new-found uncle seemed to be that the unexpected turn of events would restrain him.

Sir Oliver de Clisson was at her side. Plain knight or not, he clearly enjoyed a favoured place with the regents. She wished they would talk a little more slowly. Though she had learned French she couldn't grasp its meaning as quickly as her native Spanish. Perhaps they were plotting to have her killed before they reached Paris. They would still hold her brothers hostage even if something had happened to her.

'Surely you are not cold, princess?'

Sir Oliver leaned from his saddle to address her.

'My uncles,' she said in a low voice. 'They are enemies of my lord father.'

'But good friends to you.' His look was kind and a trifle startled. 'You do not fear them, surely?'

'I am a prisoner. When my father takes a captive — ' A searing memory of the eyeless, bloodied face at the grating made her shiver again.

'Your father's habits are not encouraged at the Court of France,' Sir Oliver said, somewhat dryly. 'You will be perfectly safe there, I promise.'

There was a reassurance about his tall, broad-shouldered frame, the curling fair hair already paling to ash. She had the treacherous thought that, if this man had been her father, she would never have woken sobbing after a ride on the nightmare.

'The convent is ten leagues further,' said her uncle of Berry, turning his head to smile at her. 'You and your dame can rest there until tomorrow and then we continue towards Paris.'

'My father — ,' she began.

'He will be informed where you and your brothers are. When he has ceased plotting against the realm his children will be returned to his custody.'

But he will never cease, Joanna thought. He has plotted thus ever since I can remember, first making treaty with one, then with another. I will never go home to Navarre again.

'I hope they give us a good meal at the convent,' Sir Oliver said. 'I ate but little before I set out. What would you like for your supper, princess?'

'The only food safe to eat when you are in the hands of your enemies is an egg,' her father had told her. 'Poison cannot be introduced into an egg.'

'I would like an egg — boiled in its shell,' she said firmly.

'Only an egg? You'll not wax fat on that!' he exclaimed laughing.

'It is all I want.' The firmness of her tone had wavered slightly. She could not go on eating eggs forever. Then a bright idea struck her. 'Unless there is a food taster,' she said.

'A food — ?' Sir Oliver's glance was full of sudden comprehension. 'Princess, you need not trouble your head about such things,' he said. 'Your uncles are just and honourable lords who loved your mother dearly and mean no harm to her children. Whatever your father chooses to do, you are in no danger.'

'But I am still a hostage,' she said sadly, and rode on again with her fair head bent.

2

'To go home?' Joanna had repeated the words slowly.

'To Navarre, to see your lord father.' His namesake of France had smiled at her. He was not a handsome man, but there was a sweetness in his face. At his side his beautiful bride, Isabeau of Bavaria, nibbled at comfits.

'I had not expected to return to Navarre,' she said. 'It is six years since I came into France. Paris seems more like my home now.'

'It gives us both pleasure to hear you say that,' Isabeau said, licking her fingers. 'If I had my way I would keep you here, but your father has signed guarantee of peace and we are obliged to return you to his custody.'

'You are fond of him, are you not?' The king gave her a slightly worried glance. 'Whatever his faults, and I pray

God they are exaggerated, he was a loving father to you, wasn't he?'

'He was never cruel,'Joanna said.

'Even the worst of men loves his children,' Charles said, looking pleased. 'I shall love mine when it is born.'

'And you are the best of men,' Isabeau said.

'I wish it were so.' He shook his head, a slight vagueness clouding his blue eyes. 'But we have lost three sons already and sometimes I wonder if the fault doesn't lie somewhere in me.'

'Many babies die before they are weaned. This coming child will live. Feel how strongly it kicks.' She took his hand, pressing it against her belly.

'A dauphin, do you think?' he asked hopefully.

'Boy or girl it will be healthy,' she replied steadily.

The vagueness had gone from his eyes and he reached with his other hand to her swelling breast.

Forgotten, Joanna made her curtsy and went out into the pleasaunce garden beyond the solar. It had been summer when she had first come to Paris, she recalled, and saw herself as she had been then, a tall, fair child, holding her feelings inside herself. She was taller now but still slender, her long hair pale gold still, her eyes the same clear hazel, her skin unblemished. Her ladies, when they dressed her, exclaimed at her beauty, declaring that no princess in Christendom was as fair as she. So far, she thought wryly, no man had said it to her, though she was close on seventeen. When men looked at her they bowed and made polite conversation, but they reserved their gallantries for other maidens. Joanna wished she knew why, but feared to ask lest she learn what she privately suspected to be the truth. Her father's evil reputation as sorcerer and poisoner was known throughout Europe, and she wondered if it had tainted her own chances.

'So you are to leave us, princess?'

She was startled out of her musings

by the approach of Sir Oliver. He must have been down at the butts. There was a bow in his hand and a fine rime of sweat at his hairline.

'To return to Navarre,' she nodded.

'And you don't wish to go?' He gave her a keen look that penetrated beyond outward courtesy.

'I don't know,' she said slowly. 'It is my duty to wish to go — '

'No, Joanna. It may be your duty to go, but wishes are not subject to duty,' he interrupted.

'But part of me wants very much to see Navarre and my lord father again,' she said with a little frown. 'Navarre is my home. I knew no other until I came here. Now I feel as if France is my home and Navarre the place I visited when I was a child.'

'I wish you could see Brittany.' He stroked the bow with his fingers as he talked and she found herself wondering how those same fingers would feel stroking her flesh. 'It is a clean, rocky, windswept land. You would like it, I think.'

'Navarre is rocky too,' she said. 'But the rocks are sun-scorched and in summer the hot wind dries up all the rivers.'

'In Brittany there are rings of stone so old that nobody knows who set them there or why,' he told her. 'You are so cool and fair the land would suit you well.'

It was a compliment and she secretly treasured it in her mind because it was the first compliment he had paid her, almost the first compliment any man had ever paid her.

'In Spain,' she said, too young and clumsy to accept it graciously, 'I was not considered much out of the common run.'

'Then the girls of Spain are lovelier than I remember,' he replied.

He was teasing her, she thought in confusion. It could be nothing more because he was older than she and a married man though he never brought his wife to Court. Yet there was a note in his voice that she had heard in other men's voices when they spoke to other women. She wanted to say something light and flirtatious back, but her tongue clove to the roof of her mouth and sweat had broken out on the palms of her hands. It was no wonder she had not yet been betrothed, she thought, when she could never think of anything clever or amusing to say to a man.

'You are very sweet, princess,' he said slowly, and the teasing had gone from his voice. He had leant the bow against the wall and, somehow or other, her hands were in his and he bent his head, kissing her on the lips. It was a long kiss, time enough for her to savour the touch of his mouth, the maleness of his scent, and then one of the other ladies came round the corner and paused, and the moment was gone as if it had never been. He dropped her hands and took a pace back, reaching for his discarded bow, sketching a salute to the newcomer before he walked away.

'I didn't realise you had an admirer in the Court.' The other girl looked amused.

'We are old friends, no more,' Joanna said stiffly, hating the other for intruding. She was not sure what would have happened next and now she would never know.

'Best keep it from His Grace,' the other warned. 'He likes the ladies of the household to be pious as nuns.'

'I am not a lady of the household!' Joanna retorted, finding some spirit. 'I am princess of Navarre and cousin german to King Charles.'

'Then he would like it even less, my dear, to learn you were dallying with a knight,' the other remarked, and flounced off before Joanna could answer her or remember her name. She started after her, biting her lip. The moment was spoiled now but a remnant of its sweetness lingered on her lips.

Three days later she began the journey to Navarre again. It was like running backwards through time to be escorted to the coast by her uncles of Berry and Burgundy, to board a ship very much like the one on which she had sailed to France. She half expected to find herself shrinking down into a little girl once more. She had not seen Sir Oliver. Common sense told her that he probably had business elsewhere, but in some part of herself she nursed the hope that he had left the Court because he could not bear to witness her departure.

At parting the King and Queen had embraced her tenderly.

'You will visit us again as soon as you can?' Charles had urged. 'We shall wish to see as much of you as we can even though you go so far. We shall greet you as a guest next time, not as a hostage.'

'Never was a hostage more kindly treated, Sire,' she answered gratefully.

'And when you come again I shall

be slim,' Isabeau declared.

'Or carrying another, eh?' Charles gave his wife a loving glance.

'Let us get this birthing over with first,' she had said, a trace of irritation in her voice. Perhaps bearing a babe was not quite the pleasure some men seemed to imagine, Joanna thought, but there was no doubt the babe would be greatly loved, whether dauphin or princess. For some reason that thought made her feel very sad. At the last moment she wanted to plead and weep like a child and beg them to allow her to stay at the Court of France and not return into Spain at all, but a princess of sixteen couldn't possibly behave in such a way, so she mastered her emotions and left them so coolly that nobody watching would have guessed that she minded in the least.

The voyage was as uneventful as her previous one had been. Her dame, older and greyer but still as landlocked as ever, declared that even the Bay of Biscay kept its temper when the princess sailed, and she noticed one or two sailors crossing their fingers and whispering as she went by. No doubt they imagined that she had inherited her father's occult gifts, she thought, and smiled inwardly.

She rode to Pamplona, and, with every step her horse took, she could feel herself being drawn more and more deeply into the red-rock fastness of Navarre. After the leafy gardens and tiny, grey-walled courtyards of Paris she had forgotten the fierce heat of the ploughed lands, carrion crows wheeling over the rocks, the dwellings of mud and stone from which the occasional peasant, bolder than the rest, crept to peep at the cavalcade riding by.

She had not expected her father to greet her, but he sent for her less than an hour before she had changed her gown, and she felt her heart beating quickly in the old jerky way as she shook the folds of her skirt into place and tried to check that her coif was on straight and that no wisp of hair straggled from her braids.

He was in his private chamber and her first thought was, 'How old he has grown!' She had never thought of her father as being of any particular age, but now it was borne in upon her that he looked his years and more, the bones of his face clearly outlined under the greyish skin, his eyes fallen back into their sockets but with the same reddish gleam behind the pupils. His hand was as cold as she remembered and shook perceptibly as she extended it for her kiss.

'So you are back from captivity.' His eyebrows arched at her.

Captivity? Even as she nodded her mind rejected the word. She felt more of a captive within these walls than she had ever felt in France.

'Did they steal your tongue away while you were in Paris?' He sank back into his chair, motioning her to rise.

'No, my lord father,' she said hastily.

'Then favour us with the latest gossip from the Court of France,' he invited.

'Queen Isabeau is with child,' Joanna said.

'Then let us hope that the King is not the father,' he remarked, 'or the babe will stand an excellent chance of growing up a halfwit.'

'Father!' Shocked, she stared at him.

'Don't tell me you lived at the French Court for six years without realising Charles is mad,' he retorted.

'His Grace had an attack of — of brain inflammation a year or two since,' she stammered.

'Is that what they call it? My dear, His Grace of France had very little brain to get inflamed,' he said impatiently. 'There's a strain of madness in the De Valois blood that comes out sooner or later. It will come out in my cousin of France more and more as the years go by until he ends as a drooling idiot, and his Bavarian Queen will find her pleasure elsewhere. Rumour says she already does so.'

'I cannot think it,' Joanna protested.

'Ah, how sweet it is to be so young

and innocent!' His voice mocked her. 'Dangerous too, my dear. Have I not taught you to trust nobody? Did you so quickly forget all you had been taught or was De Clisson teaching you new arts?'

Appalled, she stared at him, her mind racing. Only that nameless lady had seen the one kiss they'd shared. She could have sworn there'd been no other witnesses.

'Do close your mouth, Joanna. You look as witless as your Cousin Charles,' her father said.

He must have divined it, she thought wildly, through his occult powers.

'Did you fancy,' he enquired, amused, 'that I have no spies in the Courts of Europe? And not only in France are matters not quite what they seem between royal bedfellows. In England Richard of Bordeaux makes excuses for his lack of heirs, when the world knows he has never bedded his queen in her life but takes his pleasures with his own sex. It is his uncle John of Gaunt who is his staunchest ally, but Gaunt has a son who may topple Richard from his throne when his daddy is dead. But you will have heard nothing of that. I suppose you were too busy dallying with Sir Oliver.'

'He was gallant and spoke to me kindly,' she said, flushing deeply. 'There was no more to it than that.'

'Had there been,' he answered, 'you may rest assured I would have known of it, and De Clisson would now be incapable of pleasuring any woman. So! you have discovered the lure of the flesh. How fortunate that I have arranged a marriage for you that will keep such tastes within sanctioned bounds.'

'I am to be married? I was not told,' she began.

'My dear child, I am telling you now,' he said to her patiently. 'You surely didn't think I would keep you spinster for the rest of your life, did you? John of Brittany has offered for you and I have accepted.'

'Surely the Duke of Brittany is already wed?' she queried.

'Newly widowed. His second wife, Jane Holland, died recently and John seeks another mate. So far he has been unfortunate. He lost his first wife within a year or two of the nuptials and was married to the Lady Jane for less than ten. Let us hope you are of more durable material.'

'Surely he is old,' she said.

'Late fifties, I believe, but in the prime of life. He will expect many children, Joanna. Let us hope you are fertile.'

So she would go to the clean, windswept land of Brittany after all, she thought. There was consolation in that. It was probable that Sir Oliver would be a neighbour. She would be glad to see a familiar face, she decided, and tried not to remember his lips pressed against her own. The caress itself had been innocent, but the feelings it had engendered in her had not been so childlike.

'In three months' time you will sail to Brittany.' Her father winced suddenly as if some fierce pain gripped him.

'You are not well!' she exclaimed.

'I have the ague.' He controlled a shiver that racked him. 'There is nowhere one can get warm. The sun glares but does not heat. Even the flames of the fire grow cold when I stretch my hands to them.'

'There are potions and — '

'Potions and poppycock! Don't you think I have tried every remedy known to man and the devil!' he said irritably. 'However, now that you are home again I will, at least, have something to help me forget the pain. I hope you have not forgotten the instruction I gave you in certain matters not known to the majority of men?'

'It has been a long time,' she said, and thought almost wearily of the foul-smelling vials, the endless grinding of powders and steeping of herbs, the incantations to be muttered beneath the breath, the dark of the moon —

'I shall find out tomorrow when we begin our lessons again.'

'I hope I won't disappoint you,' she said meekly.

'Everyone I ever knew always disappointed me,' he returned. 'But you have, so far, disappointed me less than most. Go to your chamber now. We'll meet tomorrow.'

He had spoken kindly to her. Perhaps, deep down, where other men had a heart, he had a spark of affection for her. She tried to feel some corresponding emotion towards him in herself, but could only wonder how he knew that Sir Oliver had kissed her. A spy, no doubt, but why should he set spies on her at all?

She had not known how much she would miss Paris until she was once more in Navarre. At the French Court she had been a captive treated as a daughter. At Pamplona she was a daughter treated as a captive. Obediently pacing behind her father as she went to the laboratory where he carried out his experiments, she thought wistfully of the gaieties of the six years she had spent in France. Her uncles had been always kind and considerate to her, never reproaching her for what they saw as her father's crimes — she supposed that they were crimes, though she hoped they had been exaggerated in the telling. The King, though a trifle vague at times, had never treated her with less than perfect courtesy and she was sure his queen loved him. But her father insisted she look at life through his own distorting mirror and, when she looked, it seemed that everybody in the world was a trifle crooked after all.

It was late autumn when she set sail and the scorched plains of Navarre were lashed by an icy wind that whipped the off-shore waves into a fury. This time the Bay of Biscay lived up to its reputation, and the craggy shoreline of Brittany was in view by the time she had recovered sufficiently to set foot on deck.

'We land at Nantes, do we not?' She

forced a smile, resisting the urge to retch as the boat lurched towards the harbour.

'My Lord Duke has said that he will meet you and conduct you personally to the castle,' one of her escorts answered.

She must pinch some colour into her cheeks then and put on a more becoming mantle. She managed another wan smile as the boat lurched again and the rocky coastline crept closer.

He was waiting for her on the shore and her first impression was that her father had been teasing her, for this tall gentleman, wings of silver in his dark hair, was surely not past middle age. Even when she stood close enough to see the lines in his face, he still struck her as handsome. In youth he must have been magnificent, she thought, beginning her curtsy, but he took her hands in his, drawing her upright again.

'Your father was wrong when he described you as fair,' he said. 'You are a very lovely girl, my dear, and I am fortunate to be given such a bride.'

He had a pleasant speaking voice. Joanna, who had always been sensitive to noise, found herself liking him more and more. His hands were warm and his eyes, when they rested on her, were admiring. She had never admitted to herself that she had feared this moment, but, now that it was safely behind her, she could smile at her own foolishness.

'It is but a short ride and your palfrey is gentle.' He nodded towards a dappled mare being led forward by another member of the party and her eyes widened in delighted recognition.

'Sir Oliver! I thought you in Paris.' She held out her hand, aware of a little ripple of pleasure along her nerves as he kissed it.

'I could not remain in Paris when the prettiest lady in Christendom was coming to my own country,' he murmured, smiling.

'You must beware of Sir Oliver,' the Duke said, shaking his head. 'He is schooled in all the arts of love and will steal you away if you are not cautious.'

'A lady must be willing to be stolen away,' she retorted, 'and this lady is not.'

'You have your answer, De Clisson.' The Duke clapped him upon the shoulder. 'Make pretty speeches to your own wife and leave me to enjoy my bride! Come Joanna, I'll help you mount.'

She was a tall girl, but he swung her up to the saddle as if she had been a feather, and leapt to his own horse with agility. She was too inexperienced to guess that a man about to wed a lady young enough to be his granddaughter would take pains to appear less than his actual years.

'Where are the great stones you told me about?' she enquired of Sir Oliver, as they began to ride along the shore road.

'At Carnac. I will show them to you one day.' He was riding close, so close that his knee almost touched her leg. She felt again the little ripple of pleasure.

'When we've invaded England and taught Richard a lesson,' John of Brittany said.

'You would support France, my lord?' She felt a momentary surprise having heard that he had received his knightly training in the household of John of Gaunt.

'I support the man with the better claim,' he answered. 'I married two English wives and was happy with both, and I count Gaunt's son as like my own, but the Salic Law runs in France and it is right that a Valois sits upon the throne.'

'My Lord Duke has acted always upon his principles,' Sir Oliver said.

'And found it no bad rule of life,' the duke answered. 'Edward of England repected that in me and I hope his grandson is of the same mind, though Richard will never be the man his grandsire was or his father either.'

'They say his queen is sick,' Sir Oliver said.

'Of what malady?' the duke enquired.

'A cough, a chill.' He shrugged.

'The king adores her and will be distraught if any evil befalls her.'

'Adoration or not,' the duke said dryly, ''tis very certain that Anne of Bohemia will never die in childbed.'

Over her head the two men exchanged smiles. Riding between them Joanna suddenly felt very young.

3

She had not realised that it would be so cold during the winter. In Paris one was sheltered by the walls of the city, but here in Vannes the castle looked out over a featureless expanse of windswept rock out of which the buildings of the town, built of the same rock, could scarcely be discerned. The castle itself was much smaller that the ones in which she had spent her childhood, its furnishings austere. She had looked in vain for some feminine touch, for some echo of John's two previous wives, but there was not even a book or a scrap of embroidery to hint they had once existed.

'You must tell me what you need, my dear,' he had said, 'and I will make shift to obtain it for you. As for me I was bred to war and have lived always as a soldier.'

What she needed, she thought, was colour, great swathes of crimson, turquoise and gold to challenge the grey. The land, the sky and the sea blended into one another and she craved variety. It was foolish and ungrateful of her to feel so. The Duke was a kindly husband, if an unimaginative one, and she knew he tried to amuse her, but the difference in their ages was too great. At the end of the day he wanted to sit by the fire and talk about old campaigns, and there were no balls or state banquets to enliven the long evenings. At first she had greatly enjoyed riding to the shore to hunt for shells and stones on the pebbled beach, to look across the heaving expanse of water that looked now the colour of the rocks but, under the autumn sunlight, had sparkled into a thousand jewelled shades. But the physician had advised her not to ride and even if he had not, John would have forbidden it. This was the first of his marriages to yield fruit, and he was solicitous for the welfare of his unborn heir.

'Though if it is a girl I shall not love her the less,' he assured Joanna. 'The one after will be a boy, I am certain.'

He was so eager to make her happy that it would have been churlish to have grumbled about the weather, the lack of entertainment. There were many compensations too. The servants were dark-browed Bretons, speaking a patois quite different from the French she had learned, but it was clear that they respected the duke and were anxious to welcome his young bride. When she took an occasional walk there was always a little group of them to present flowers or fresh cheese — poor enough gifts for the blossoms were sparse and the cheese sour on the tongue, but given with a kindliness that touched her deeply. And Sir Oliver rode over frequently to visit her, bringing with him snippets of gossip to enliven the monotony.

'Queen Isabeau is delivered of a

daughter whom they will name Isabella. They say the child is healthy and very pretty, save that she has the King's nose.'

Which gave the lie to her father's insinuations, Joanna thought, pleased. She had written to him with word of her own pregnancy, but had as yet received no reply though she knew that the duke had received a letter from Navarre. He had gone to his own rooms to peruse it and, immediately afterwards, called for his groom and gone riding. As she chatted with Sir Oliver, she found herself wondering if the letter had contained ill tidings of her father's health. It was ironic that all his secret knowledge couldn't cure his own various ailments.

'You look well, madam.'

Her thoughts had strayed a little and she realised that her visitor's manner had warmed, his voice deepening. Nothing improper had ever passed between them, but she sensed he had not forgotten that kiss in the garden of

Paris, and that there were times when he wished it might be repeated. He had not yet brought his wife to wait upon her, it being generally known that Lady de Clisson was not strong, but Joanna, though she told herself firmly that Sir Oliver was no more than a good friend, was in no particular hurry to meet the lady.

'I feel well,' she answered, 'but I wish I could take more exercise. I would like to see more of Brittany.'

'After the babe is born I will keep my promise and offer myself as an escort on your trip to Carnac,' he said at once.

'I look forward to it.' She held out her hand to him impulsively and he caught it in both his own and said, in a low voice from which all trace of Court gallantry had fled, 'If you were not John of Brittany's wife.'

'Sir Oliver, you must not speak so.' She withdrew her hand and went over to the fire pulling her mantle more closely round her.

What he would have said or done next would remain a matter for speculation, for a step beyond the door was followed by the entrance of the Duke. He was still booted and spurred and there was a curious air of suppressed excitement about him as if he had reached some far-reaching decision.

'Sir Oliver! The very person I wanted to see!'

His greeting was hearty, but something was amiss. She knew it instinctively though she was not sure how she knew. Perhaps it was her own confusion that made her fancy his voice was a shade too loud, his smile too jocular.

'I was not aware you were from home, my lord.' Sir Oliver evidently noticed nothing amiss, for he answered easily with no trace of embarrassment. 'I came to enquire when you intend to call your Council.'

'In a day or two. I had another matter on which I wanted to consult you.'

'I am at your disposal,' Sir Oliver said equably.

'Ah! I am fortunate in the loyalty of my vassals.' The Duke clapped him upon the shoulder. 'It is about my castle of Ermine.'

'It is a ruin, sir.'

'You need not tell me so!' The duke grimaced: 'I have promised myself for years to put it right, for the walls reproach me every time I pass by them. The foundations and the tower are structurally sound, but a new moat will need to be dug, more rooms added. It will provide better accommodation for my wife and child.'

'We are to move?' Joanna felt a little startled.

'Ermine will make a fine summer residence,' the Duke said. For some reason his eyes avoided hers, though the smile on his face was genial. 'I want you to ride over with me there, Oliver, and give me your opinion.'

'I am no architect, my lord,' Sir Oliver protested.

'But Ermine is built on the same lines as your own place,' the Duke said. 'You had some improvements made there a year or two since.'

'To please my lady wife.'

'Which is what I hope to do at Ermine. Come! the day's still young enough and darkness has not yet fallen. Sieur Bazvalen has the keys to the castle.'

He had his hand on the other's arm and was urging him out. His movement was friendly, almost as if they were equals. There was no need for Joanna to feel the sudden dread at her heart. Yet it lingered after the two men had clattered down the stairs. The physician had told her that pregnant women sometimes had strange fancies. She hoped that he was right and that the uneasiness coursing through her was no more than a symptom of her condition.

In an attempt to calm herself she went down the stairs and across the courtyard to the tiny chapel. In France she had attended Mass every morning in the royal chapel and spent most of her time admiring the fine hangings and jewel-encrusted statues with which it was decorated. In Navarre, though she had gone to service with her father, the knowledge that he went only for custom's sake and had no real belief in what he termed mummery had tinged her own attitude with scepticism. But here at Vannes she had discovered to her surprise that the tiny chapel drew and held her interest. It was so small that, when the entire household was gathered, half of them had to stand outside.

Within there were a few benches, an altar of carved stone with a bronze crucifix hanging above it and, in one corner, a wooden statue of the Madonna — not a smug, bejewelled Virgin but a girl with sabots on her feet, her hands joined together, a look on her stolid peasant features of puzzled wonderment as if she had heard the beating of enormous wings.

With this Virgin Joanna could feel a sense of kinship. She sat down on one of the benches, pulling her mantle more snugly about her thickening figure, and bowed her head, repeating silently a prayer for protection, though she was not sure what threatened her. Perhaps it was, after all, only the nebulous fancy of a pregnant woman.

Evening drew in, darkness falling early at this end of the year. She left the chapel, not much comforted, as the old priest was bringing in the tapers, and went back to the chamber above the hall where the Duke liked to sit with her sometimes when the day was coming to an end. It was good of him to bear her company when she suspected he would much prefer to be with his knights, quaffing malmsey and making men's boasts. He was a good husband and there was no reason for her to feel this lonely dread tightening steel bands round her heart.

It was long past suppertime when she heard his footsteps on the stairs and her feeling of relief died away when he entered, for his face was set in hard lines, all the geniality gone.

'My lord, I began to fear some accident had befallen you!' She rose swiftly to greet him, aware that her voice was pitched a shade higher than usual. 'I waited supper for you.'

'You should have eaten,' he said brusquely. 'I have no appetite.'

'I thought perhaps — you might have brought guests with you.' Her voice trailed away uncertainly as he turned towards her.

'If you mean Sir Oliver,' he said, 'he has no appetite either. In fact Sir Oliver will never have an appetite again.'

'I don't understand. Has there been an accident?' She backed a little away, staring at him.

'De Clisson is dead, at my orders,' he said flatly, and turned to pour wine into a goblet on a nearby table.

'Dead? But how? Why? I don't understand.' She felt the blood rushing from her face and caught at the back of a chair to steady herself.

'When we reached Ermine I invited De Clisson to go ahead of me up into the tower. I had men already waiting there to seize and pinion him. Sieur Bazvalen was ordered to dispatch him at once and so I came away.'

He drained the goblet at a draught and thumped it down upon the table.

'You have had Sir Oliver killed?' The vague dread that had been troubling her took shape and substance. 'In the name of God, why?'

'Perhaps you can guess the reason, Madam?' His voice was cold.

'There *is* no reason to kill a faithful friend!' She cried in agitation. 'Sir Oliver was a faithful friend and loyal vassal to you.'

'And to you? What was he to you?'

'To me?' Her face was white, she stared at him.

'Aye, to you. Is it not true that he was in love with you, that you were recalled from the Court of France because of his importunities? Is it not so?'

'Who told you such tales? I swear to you that — '

'Your father writes to me from Navarre. Read for yourself!' He thrust a letter beneath her nose, pointing to a paragraph near the end of the closely written sheet. The handwriting blurred and wavered, then stood out black and clear.

'The news of the coming babe pleases me. It is good for a young wife to breed early lest her mind become bored and her hands ripe for mischief. Neither need you fear that the child is not yours. Joanna gave no encouragement to the advances of Sir Oliver de Clisson though, knowing him to be a smooth-tongued rogue, I took the precaution of recalling her to Navarre lest her sympathies be roused.'

Charles of Navarre had not forgiven that kiss exchanged in the garden of the French Court. She raised her head and stared at her husband, her hazel eyes clear and searching, but it was of her father she was thinking. So much had been made clear in a few seconds. When she spoke her voice was low, throbbing with truth.

'My lord father makes false insinuations. They call him Charles the Bad and it is a name well earned, though it shames me to say so. Everything good and clean he spoils, for the pleasure of spoiling it. When I was small he kept me with him and I wondered if it was because he loved me best, but I think now it was because he never loved me at all, nor wished me to love anyone else. It is not true that Sir Oliver, or any other man, importuned me. He was polite and kind to me because I was a stranger and a hostage, and he has been my good friend since. My father received word from me that I am happy with you and carry your child, so he cannot rest until he spoils that too, and makes enmity instead of amity between us. You have had an innocent man killed.'

She finished speaking, biting her lip hard to keep from sobbing, seeing the seasoned warrior before her dwindle into a middle-aged man fearful lest he failed to retain his hold upon his young wife's affections.

'You speak the truth? Sir Oliver did not seek to — ?'

'Never,' she answered firmly, and tossed a bundle of might-have-beens through the window.

'Lord God, what have I done?' The Duke sat down abruptly, covering his face with his hands.

'You have killed an innocent man,' Joanna repeated. At that moment she hated him as much as she hated her father for marrying her to him.

'I will do penance,' the duke began, and broke off miserably. 'It is my temper,' he said at last and shook his head. 'I have always been of a choleric temper. I was bred to war, to attack and defence, and my reactions are very quick, I fear! I was ever one to strike first and beg pardon afterwards.'

'But it is not my pardon you must beg,' she said, gently, inexorably.

'I never blamed you,' he said quickly, 'though I confess I did wonder if you had given him — unwittingly, some encouragement.'

'None,' she answered stonily, 'for he made no overtures. My father lied to you. To set people against one another is his way of amusing himself.'

'I must go to Ermine again.' He rose, looking so weary that had she not been so sick at heart she would have pitied him. 'An honourable burial?' He had paused, gazing at her. At the back of his eyes was the unspoken hope that, even now, there might be some justification for the murder.

'Sir Oliver was an honourable man,' she said stiffly. 'He deserves no less.'

He went without another word, descending the steps outside with the heavy tread of an ageing, repentant man. It was not his fault, she thought fiercely. It was her father who had reached out grimy fingers from Navarre and sought to plant suspicions in his mind, and he had acted swiftly, treacherously to set aside a fancied rival. The Duke too, for all that he chided himself for quick temper, had not struck out in blind fury. He had invited Sir Oliver under the guise of friendship, to visit castle Ermine where men had been waiting.

After what seemed like a long time she went to her own chamber. There were tapers already burning there and a sleepy maidservant tended the fire. Joanna dismissed her and took up an unused taper, holding it close to the heat until it began to soften shaping it into the rough resemblance of a human figure, the words of incantation dropping gently from her lips.

It was nearly dawn by the time the task was finished. The basin in which she had burned the waxen figure was scorched and black, and her eyelids were heavy from lack of sleep. It was the first time she had used the knowledge, and the hatred was all burned out of her. What was done was done, and regret was as foolish as loving. She washed her face and tidied her hair, and went down into the courtyard where a fine mist of rain obscured the walls and the gatehouse. A tall figure, accompanied by a couple of knights, was riding in. She stood on the steps of the hall, waiting for him to dismount.

'My dear child, you are up early!' The Duke put his arm about her shoulder as they went indoors.

'I could not sleep.' She made no attempt to dislodge the arm.

'God be praised, no harm has been done!' His low voice was exultant. 'Sieur Bazvalen had not yet carried out my order. He knows me better than I know myself, for he guessed I would think twice of my hasty decision! Sir Oliver was alive but fettered. I ordered his release, though I fear he was less than grateful.'

'Oh?' She moved out of the shadow

of his arm and shot him a questioning look.

'He declares himself ill used and claims compensation. Compensation! As if I had money to burn! We argued most of the night and at the last he rode away, declaring himself to be a man ill used.'

'He spoke truly,' Joanna said.

'Perhaps so, but where there is smoke — ' The Duke frowned. She guessed that he still hoped for some justification of the attempted murder. He caught her eye and said hastily, 'I do not disbelieve you, my love, but on De Clisson's part there might have been intent. Else why should your father have fixed upon him rather than anybody else?'

'Who knows the workings of my father's mind?' she countered.

'And he is a sick man, they say.' He was turning over possibilities in his head. 'Well, De Clisson has ridden to Paris. He declares he will complain of his mistreatment to Charles. I fear it will cause trouble between France and Brittany. The Valois is swayed by every wind that blows. I am half minded to lend my support to England after all.'

It was a sombre harvest to be reaped from a kiss in a garden, she thought bitterly, and yawned.

'If you will excuse me, my lord, I believe I did rise too early,' she said.

'Go back to bed and rest for a few hours.' His expression was anxious and kindly. 'We must remember the babe.'

But he had not remembered it when he had told her so abruptly that Sir Oliver was dead. She gave him a vague smile and drifted out. Whatever had been set in motion would take its course, and there was nothing to be done but wait.

The waiting was not long. Shortly after Yuletide, which she had spent quietly, word reached them from Navarre.

'It appears that your father, seeking some relief from the pains in his joints, gave orders that he was to be bound tightly in sheets soaked in wine and spices. This was done, but a candle overturned in the wind and his wrappings ignited — a truly terrible way to die, my love, and you must try not to dwell upon it too greatly.'

'My father always complained of the cold,' Joanna said. 'In the end he had heat enough, it seems.'

'My love!' John of Brittany looked so shocked that she would have laughed had she not felt so dismal.

'I jest merely not to weep,' she said hurriedly.

'A terrible end, indeed,' he said, 'though many in Europe will say it was not undeserved. We must offer many masses for his soul.'

They would avail him nothing, she thought stonily. By now Charles of Navarre would probably be roasting in hell.

'I hope he knows,' she thought with sudden venom, 'that I was the one who sent him there.'

He had left her his library and some

pearls that had belonged to her mother. They were to be packed up and sent to Brittany, and her brother, whom she scarcely knew, would be crowned King as soon as his lip service had been paid to mourning. There was no reason for her ever to return to Navarre. Neither was it likely that she would see France again in the near future.

'De Clisson has demanded full restitution for what he terms wrongful arrest and the Valois supports his claim,' the Duke said wrathfully. 'He will cause a civil war within my own borders!'

'Cannot you make restitution?' she asked wearily.

'And lose face before my allies? Don't be foolish, Joanna.'

'Surely it is even more foolish for a nation to go to war because two men have had a falling-out,' she countered.

'You are young and female, so cannot understand these things.' His annoyed tone became irritatingly forbearing. 'War frightens ladies. You will feel more yourself after the child is born.'

Whatever that is supposed to mean, she thought, submitting to his caress. The truth was that there were times when she wasn't certain of her identity at all, times when the pale, pretty face above the swollen body seemed the face of a stranger. Perhaps he was right and she would be better after the baby was born, but she knew already that she could never again be the girl in the garden.

4

'Is it true,' asked Jean-Pierre, who was of an enquiring turn of mind, 'that people change completely every seven years?'

'I'm sure I don't know, dear.' Joanna, giving a final tweak to the veil that was stretched tightly over her wide, low headdress, gave her eldest child an affectionate glance. 'Why?'

'Because in two years' time I will be seven and I wonder if I will change.'

'Not too much, I hope. I like you very well as you are.' She reached out to pat him, but he evaded her touch with all the hauteur of a boy recently breeched.

'Better than Maria and Arthur and Jules?'

'In a different way,' Joanna said.

'Jules is foolish. He still wets himself,' Jean-Pierre said scornfully.

'So did you, when you were ten months old. Give him time and he will change too,' she told him.

'By then I will be nearly old enough to go and fight in the wars with Father.' Jean-Pierre made a feint at her with his wooden sword. 'There will still be wars, won't there?'

'I expect so. Now run along and play, there's a dear.'

He was a sweet child, but she was nearly six months pregnant again already and his boisterousness wearied her. There were times, much as she loved the children, when she wondered if the rest of her life was all going to be bearing babes and hearing talk of interminable battles. Five children in six years, if one counted the little stillborn girl delivered in the spring after her father's death. Seeing the white, dead flower-face she had wondered if this was God's punishment on her for the night she had used the secret knowledge.

She had resolved then never to use it again even on those who deserved it, and the next four children were all healthy and sturdy. Three boys and a girl and, from the way she was carrying, she guessed this would be another boy. Richard was a good name and would be a pretty compliment to Richard of England.

Thinking of him she sighed briefly. She had never laid eyes on the Plantagenet, though she had heard he was handsome. Men might whisper he was a boy-lover, but he had adored his wife so much that, at her death, he had set fire to her favourite palace of Shene with his own hands. Part of her envied the emotion that could have given rise to such a grandly romantic gesture. Part of her shivered at the thought of tapestries, plate, furnishings, going up in smoke. England was a wealthy country, they said, and Richard an extravagant monarch, but even so — ! With a restless discontent, she found herself looking round the room. There was no denying that it was shabby. The arras was torn and faded, flapping in the breeze that came through the unglassed window, and the loose robe she wore had already seen her through three of her pregnancies.

'The wars cost a very great deal, my dear,' the Duke had informed her the last time she had asked for an increase in her allowance. 'Most of my revenue must be spent on the defence of the realm.'

'If you did not quarrel with everybody,' she retorted sharply, 'there would be no need to take these extraordinary precautions against attack.'

'You do not understand these matters,' he had answered.

Joanna thought that she understood them very well. The husband who had never given her or their children an impatient word was constitutionally unable to live on peaceful terms with either his neighbours or his vassals. He enjoyed conflict more than he enjoyed negotiation, and on the rare occasions when all was peaceful he generally started a quarrel simply for amusement's sake. He grudged new gowns and furnishings, but would happily spend on cannon balls and pikes and mercenaries.

With a sudden decision in her face, Joanna rose from the mirror and went down the steps into the great hall. As usual the Duke, surrounded by his henchmen, was retelling some old campaign or perhaps plotting a new one — as far as Joanna was concerned one battle ran into the next and all were equally tedious in the telling.

'My lord, I wish to talk with you.' She interrupted the flow of narrative without compunction.

'I was explaining how we deployed our forces at the battle of Aurey,' he began.

'It's important,' Joanna said firmly.

'In that case, gentlemen, we must yield to the fair sex.' He waved a dismissal, trying not to sound reluctant. Joanna was a good wife and a fruitful one, and he supposed it only natural that a woman in her condition should nag a little.

'It is about money,' Joanna said.

'I thought it might be.' The Duke sighed. 'You cannot have spent your allowance already!'

'I regret so.' There was a faint tinge of sarcasm in her voice. 'It is a little difficult to make it stretch far enough to cover my garments and the children's shoes and the dame's wages *and* new bolsters for the bed.'

'You do wonders,' he said hastily.

'But it ought not to be necessary for me to have to do wonders,' she said. 'John, I am Duchess of Brittany, not a merchant's wife. I ought not to have to scrimp and save, and wear gowns three seasons old. All your revenues are spent on campaigns, and the campaigns only arise because you ceaselessly intrigue — first with England against France, then with France against England. And always against De Clisson, though he is the one who should bear a grudge against you.'

'It was De Clisson who raised rebellion against me and complained to the Valois.'

'Because you had ordered his death and, the instant he went into France, you seized all his property, and in all the years since you have refused to meet him or talk truce.'

'You plead for De Clisson?' He gave her a frowning look.

'For myself. I plead for myself.' She had seated herself opposite him and now she leaned forward, her hazel eyes darkening with the intensity of her convictions. 'John, if you keep up this stupid feud, the day will come when people may start to suspect that there was some truth in my father's lies. My reputation could suffer because of something that never happened!'

'Never for one moment did I ever dream that you encouraged him,' he protested.

'Yet the quarrel continues, tearing our land apart. John, good men are being killed on both sides simply because Sir Oliver de Clisson *didn't* try to seduce me! The children and I are cooped up here at Vannes and there is never enough money. Even the servants go unpaid because your campaigns eat up the revenues! There has to be an end to it somewhere!'

'I was bred to war,' he said stubbornly.

'But you will not always be here to make war!' She used an argument she hoped she would never have to use. 'You are past sixty and, though I pray God to grant you many years of good health yet, there is always the possibility that you will leave me a widow with my children still small. Do you want me to be without friends when you are gone? France and England will tear Brittany apart if she is still divided at your death and Jean-Pierre will have a bitter inheritance.'

'What is it you want?' The words dragged out of him, but she sensed that her remarks had struck home.

'Make peace with Sir Oliver and the rest of the rebel vassals,' she urged.

'Leave your son a land that is not torn apart by warring factions. Meet with De Clisson and make peace, for my sake and the children's sake!'

'You are eloquent, Joanna.' There was weariness as well as affection in his voice.

'Because I am tired of being poor,' she said. 'Brittany spends her time fighting, instead of trading. If we make the right alliances we could hold the balance between France and England. We achieve nothing while we are fighting among ourselves!'

'You have developed political instincts,' he said. 'I married a child and find my wife is a statesman.'

'Will you meet with De Clisson?'

'I will suggest it.' There was a flash of the old jealousy in his face. 'Perhaps you desire to see him again yourself.'

'Not unless you think it necessary,' she answered coolly. 'The quarrel is between you and him. My own feelings were never engaged.'

It was not quite the truth, but it was

as near as she dared come. Sensing that she had said enough she leaned back, changing the subject.

'And now that we are in accord may I stay to hear something of the battle of Aurey? It is stupid of me, I know, but I never can get the details of it straight in my mind.'

It was more than a month before Sir Oliver came. He rode in with so strong an escort that some of her more timid ladies squeaked with fright, half convinced that they were about to be besieged.

From her window Joanna watched as the Duke went out to greet his guest, a mark of special courtesy which she hoped the visitor would notice. Jean-Pierre, striving to appear very grown up and important, was at his father's side. The two men bowed, exchanged a few words, turned together to enter the hall. Sir Oliver had removed his hat and, from above, she saw with surprise that he had nearly as much grey in his hair as the Duke had. Everybody in the world was growing older.

She had excused herself from the meeting, preferring not to appear when she was so near her time. She felt also that it might rouse the old hostilities if she were present. The Duke had never believed ill of her, but he might easily believe it of Sir Oliver if he saw them together. There were moments, she suspected, when he regretted not having had De Clisson's murder actually carried out.

Dismissing her ladies, whose chatterings and speculations had begun to irritate her, she took the back stairway to the chapel. At this hour it was one of the few places where she could be sure of privacy. Thin April sunlight haloed the head of the peasant Virgin and the stone walls held peace in their depths.

'My lady.'

She realised, when she heard his voice, that she had known he would find her. He walked to where she sat and stood looking at her across a little space, though she had the odd impression that he stood at a great distance.

'Sir Oliver.'

She inclined her head slightly, thinking sadly, 'But he is past middle age and looks older. I thought him so handsome when I was a girl.'

'The Duke and I have made our peace,' he said. 'It should have been made long since, but we are both stubborn men. I told him that I was coming here for a few moments' private prayer. I saw you at the window and I guessed you would seek the chapel. In France you sometimes used to go and sit in the chapel there when you were lonely or troubled.'

'That's true!' she exclaimed. 'I didn't think anyone had noticed.'

'I noticed everything about you,' he said. 'You were so shy and pale, but your hair was bright as the sun and when you smiled little flecks of gold danced in your eyes. Had I not been married or you a princess, the Duke

81

might have had good reason to kill me. Your father was nearer the truth than he knew.'

Once his words would have meant something to her, but it was too late. He had grown elderly and she was the mother of a family, and there was no garden.

'I am glad there is truce,' she said lightly. 'I would have Brittany strong and prosperous for my son's sake. Now, if you will excuse me, I'll leave you to your prayers.'

He would have kissed her hand, but she evaded his touch, inclining her head and sweeping past him. Everything in her wanted to weep, most of all because there was nothing to weep about, there never having been anything between them.

The child — a boy, as she had expected — was born with the same ease and rapidity as the others at the beginning of summer, and was named Richard as she had decided, though the Duke grumbled a little.

'Surely Charles would have been more fitting, my love, since I have been persuaded to renew my allegiance to the Valois?'

'I have little cause to love the name Charles,' she answered stonily. 'My father's mischief caused great harm to me and mine, and as for the King of France — if rumour tells true, there is something wrong with his mind. I had hoped it was not so for he was always kind to me, but it seems certain that he has fits of mania.'

'I am beginning to think that Richard Plantagenet has them too,' the Duke said wryly. 'You have heard he is to marry again?'

'To whom?' Joanna looked interested.

'To Isabella of France. Aye, you may well stare, for he's past thirty and she is not yet ten! His councillors have been after him to wed since Queen Anne died, but he would have none of the ladies they suggested. Well, there's another wife he'll never bed, for, though he loved Anne, I have it on good authority that she died a virgin.'

There was no doubt about it, Joanna decided in exasperation, John, deprived of battles, was as full of gossip as a scold. Already he was off again.

'When Richard dies I'll lay odds there will be no son to follow him and that will be Henry Bolingbroke's chance. Gaunt's son won't rest until he sits upon his cousin's throne and who can blame him? He's in the prime of life with a fine family — six of them, though the last cost his wife her life, poor soul! She and Bolingbroke made a love match, they say, though I dare say the fact Mary de Bohun was the richest heiress in England made her even more attractive.'

The battle of Aurey would have been preferable, thought Joanna.

But there were no battles now. Neither was there much more money. Too much had been spent on the campaigns for luxuries to be bought.

'And as you are again with child, my

love, you will not need new gowns for a while,' the Duke said.

Richard scarcely three months old and she had quickened again. It seemed sometimes as if she had been pregnant all her life. The child Isabella was fortunate to have a betrothed who cared little for women in a physical sense but always treated them kindly — and generously. There were times, though Joanna was always ashamed of them afterwards, when she wished her husband were impotent.

The lack of money caused yet another disappointment that summer. Marie was five, a blonde miniature of her mother, with pretty taking ways. It had been hoped to betroth her to Bolingbroke's son but, at the last moment, the dowry demanded with her had been ruled out as too large.

'For Jean d'Alençon will take her for half that amount and his father gives her leave to remain with us until she is twelve and ready for the marriage.'

'Jean d'Alençon is never likely to

become King of England,' Joanna said resentfully. It was a sad state of affairs when her only daughter had to be married less brilliantly than she deserved because of the state of her father's dukedom. 'Surely we can find more.'

'Alençon is a pleasant child and will grow into a fine boy,' the Duke said. 'And you know you would fret about her were she to be married off in England. In France you will see much more of her.'

'In England she would have been richer,' Joanna muttered. It was useless to continue the discussion. The plain fact was that the dowry they contrived to scrape together was so small that Marie was lucky to receive a promise of marriage from anybody at all. Meanwhile there was nothing to be gained by quarrelling with John, who had begun to affect slight deafness when she argued anyway.

The new babe was a girl and Joanna, peering into the tiny, crumpled face, was overwhelmed as usual by a surge of tenderness. This one would be called Blanche, she decided, and when the time came she would have as large a dowry as her loving mother could devise.

She was pregnant again before three months had passed but this time, the physician warned her, must be the last.

'You have borne eight children in a scant seven years,' he reproved. 'Your health, thanks be to God, is excellent, but I cannot guarantee that it will continue so unless you leave off childbearing.'

'Best tell my husband,' she advised dryly. 'My babes are not immaculately begotten, you know.'

After so many childless years the Duke seemed determined to repopulate his duchy through his own efforts. She could almost wish for another war to turn his thoughts in a different direction. But though there were occasional rumblings of discontent from those vassals who believed themselves to be harshly treated by their warlike ruler, Brittany was quiet.

'Neither is it possible for us to hold the balance between France and England,' the Duke grumbled. 'Richard's marriage to Isabella de Valois has made peace between the two countries. He has abandoned his claim to the throne of France and is said to be on the most excellent terms with Charles. It will not please his uncle of Lancaster but Richard seems to be more interested in decking his child bride with every finery his imagination can devise.'

'Lucky Isabella,' Joanna said lightly. Word of the little bride's gifts from her bridegroom had spread through Europe.

'A mantle of scarlet velvet embroidered with gold and silver birds and another of brown sewn with seed-pearls and amber! They say that at Windsor she sleeps in a bed of ivory fashioned like a swan,' Marie said. At seven her fancy was caught by the fantastic image. 'I wish I had a bed shaped like a swan, and a red mantle with birds on it.'

'Brittany is a poor country. Your father cannot afford such things,' Joanna scolded.

'Is France rich?'

'Why, yes. When I was there the Court was kept in very great state.'

'Then why cannot I be sent to the Duc d'Alençon now? Why must I wait until I am twelve?' Marie demanded.

'Why, love, I didn't think you would wish to go so far from home until you are older,' Joanna demurred. 'Surely you would miss all of us very much?'

'Not if d'Alençon is rich,' Marie said. The child was in the right of it, Joanna reflected. Sooner or later she would have to leave her parents. Better for her to be reared in luxury than at the penny-pinching Breton Court. If her departure was delayed until she was twelve, she would find it all the harder to settle. It was selfish to keep her, but she was so small to go so far from home and she had just reached that delightful age when the world seems full of mysteries which the child eagerly questions.

'I will speak to your father,' Joanna said at last, 'and if he agrees we will send you into France.'

John would certainly agree. Where the children were concerned he trusted her judgement absolutely. Marie would be reared in France and married into a family too wealthy to care that she brought with her so tiny a dowry.

Her newest baby was another girl, much smaller than the others.

'Though she's healthy enough.' The physician, who had attended her through a longer labour than usual, handed the babe back to the midwife for swaddling and gave his patient a frowning look. 'Forgive my frankness, but how old are you?'

'Twenty-six,' Joanna said, too weary to be offended.

'This must be the last child. You look older than your years, madam, and it is a great pity for you're a comely woman.'

'Then you must speak to my husband. He is proud to have sired a family at his age.'

'Four sons and three daughters is sufficient for a man of any age,' the physician said. 'I am a husband myself but my four were born each three years apart, and my wife still has her looks and her health. The Duke must discipline himself to restrain his ardour.'

'In that case,' she said, amused, 'you had better not speak to him. He would not take such interference very kindly.'

'There are ways in which a wife may prevent conception,' the physician said, not looking at her, but examining his hands with grave attention. 'Such ways are forbidden by Holy Mother Church, but priests and nuns do not generally have children. It is possible that your ladyship may have heard of such precautions, read of them? I mention it in passing.'

He had bowed and left the chamber before she could make any reply. Joanna stared after him, her brow furrowed. Her back ached intolerably from the long hours of pushing and her breasts were already beginning to hurt. In a year, in less than a year, she would be lying in this same bed unless —

'You ought to rest, madam.' One of her waiting women had entered and was hovering solicitously.

'For a little while.' Joanna leaned back on the pillows. 'Is my lord by?'

'Drinking the babe's health down in the hall. He says he's pleased it's a little maid, but next year he's wagering on another son.'

'Is he so? Anne, you recall the books my brother sent to me after our father's death? They are still in the trunk, are they not?'

'Yes, my lady. You said to leave them there.'

'When I've rested,' Joanna said, 'have the trunk brought up here, will you? I have a fancy to do a little reading.'

5

Spring had crept upon them unawares. The lashing, rain-laden winds that gusted over the rocks had dwindled into breezes that carried with them the tang of sea-salt, and there were flowers in the cleft of the castle wall. And I, thought Joanna, am thirty years old. Middle-aged and wed to an old man who talks endlessly of the battles fought when he was young and handsome. For nearly thirteen years I have lived in a small castle in a poor land. She frowned, checking her mood of self-pity. There were many good things in her life. Her children, save for the youngest, were healthy and the physician had assured her that even Marguerite would grow stronger with care. Marie was at the French Court and growing, according to all reports, into a very pretty young girl. John, for all his prosiness, had been a kind husband, and Brittany, despite its bleakness and poverty, had its moments of fugitive charm when the wind dropped and the sun lit the grey rock into gold and blue and a subtle shading of rose.

She had looked in on the sleeping children, and seen the Duke comfortably ensconced by the fire with a cushion at his back. Now, donning a cloak, she made her way up the winding staircase to the battlements. Usually, as evening fell, she paced here for a time, trying to still her restlessness. It was not quite dark and she could see the outlines of houses sharp against the blood-red sun. Figures, tiny as ants, moved against the horizon, grew larger as they approached. A dozen riders, strung out blackly against the skyline, were heading towards Vannes. The old uneasiness gripped her and she went quickly down the stairs to check that the drawbridge was up, the night guard in position. There had been peace for a long time, but peace could so easily be shattered.

'What is it, my dear?' The Duke had been dozing in his chair, but the sound of hoofbeats must have penetrated his sleep.

'Riders coming this way.' She broke off as the captain of the guard entered.

'My lord, there are men at the postern gate, seeking admittance,' he said.

'In whose name?' John asked.

'Bolingbroke. He is banished from the French Court and seeks shelter.'

'What in thunder was Harry Bolingbroke doing at the French Court?' John demanded.

'You forget,' Joanna reminded him, 'that King Richard banished both him and Mowbray from England for seven years, and that the Earl rode to the Valois Court. Charles will not want to break the treaty with England by succouring Richard's rival.'

'Treaty or no treaty we can scarcely leave Lancaster's son to spend the night on the road,' John said. 'Bid them enter. Joanna, have we the welcome cup ready?'

'And food also.' She spoke reassuringly, mentally calculating the number of cold chickens a dozen men might eat. 'If you will excuse me — '

'Nonsense, nonsense! Stay and greet them. You have not met Gaunt's son.'

She would have appreciated time in which to change her dress, tidy herself a little, but the captain had left and she could hear the creaking of the drawbridge as it was lowered, the clattering of hooves and harness.

'My lord of Brittany, this is uncommonly kind of you.'

The man who entered was in his early thirties. He looked tired and dusty, but he carried himself well, reddish head high, shoulders wide and straight beneath his mantle. He had a broad, tanned countenance, his beard clipped short, his eyes surprisingly dark in contrast to the auburn of his colouring.

'There is always a welcome for the son of my old friend,' John said.

He had begun to rise but the younger man prevented him with a swift gesture.

'You have not heard the news then? My father died, sir Duke.'

'Died? Gaunt is dead?' John stared up at him.

'A few days since. He was ailing when I left England. My banishment — broke something in him. Richard knew it would but he didn't care. My father never swerved in his loyalty, but at the last Richard served him ill.'

'Gaunt dead.' The Duke shook his head as if the information had dazed him. 'He was younger than I am.'

'The youngest of Edward's sons.' The Earl nodded. 'He often spoke of you, of his old friend.'

'Aye, we were knights together. A long time ago.' The Duke shook his head again and turned to where Joanna stood. 'The welcome cup, my dear.'

She took it from the servant and

stepped forward with it. She had not had time to remove her cloak and it fell away from her white arms to reveal her tall, ripe figure in a manner more flattering to her than she realised.

'Welcome, my lord Earl.' She hesitated, then added, 'I too will add my regrets to those of my husband. I have heard much of your late father and often wished to meet him.'

'My lady.' He bowed and took the cup, draining it thirstily.

'Sit down, sit down.' John shifted in his chair, sending the cushion at his back spinning. 'I have a touch of ague tonight. The curse of old age, I fear.'

'And the damp season which is no respecter of persons,' Bolingbroke said tactfully, taking the adjacent chair. 'I have known the cramps of ague myself when I was on campaign.'

'Ah, campaign!' There was a wistful note in the Duke's voice. In a moment, Joanna thought, he will begin to talk of Aurey.

'There is some supper on the way,'

she interposed. 'Your escort is being quartered in the guard-room, but you may prefer to eat here by the fire. Then the Duke and you may talk.'

'You also, madam. I am not one who excludes women from my Councils,' he said.

'Oh, my wife's a sensible woman with a good head on her shoulders,' the Duke said. 'I have been fortunate in my spouse.'

'As I was in mine.' There was a tinge of sadness in Bolingbroke's voice. The story of his having wed Mary de Bohun for love must have been true.

'A sad loss,' Joanna said conventionally.

'Sad indeed.' He frowned. 'It is nearly six years since she died and every new death reminds me of hers. But she gave me a fine family, as you have given to your lord.'

'They are in England still?'

'At my father's house. When I was banished he undertook to care for them. I did not know that his guardianship was destined to last less than six months.'

'You have plans?' The Duke leaned forward in his chair, looking more wide awake.

'Nebulous ones.' Bolingbroke accepted a plate of meat and began to eat rapidly. 'When I left England I promised my father that I would obey King Richard and serve out my exile of seven years. His death changes that. I will not wait seven years before I embrace my children or see England again.'

'You will return without leave?' Joanna stared at him.

'If I wait seven years Richard will have ruined everything our grandfather achieved during his long reign,' the other said tensely. 'He cares nothing for England or good government or the honour of his House. His father's conquests mean nothing to him, less than nothing, for he is perfectly ready to hand back all that the Black Prince won. My royal cousin is more interested in balls than battles!'

Joanna, listening, couldn't help but feel a sneaking sympathy with the absent Richard, but the Duke snorted.

'The lad was spoiled by his mother,' he pronounced. 'Joan of Kent, God rest her, was a sweet lady but something of a fool. In her eyes the boy could do no wrong.'

'He is not a boy, my lord, any longer,' Bolingbroke said. 'He is past thirty and we can wait no longer for him to grow up and act like a king.'

'I smell rebellion,' the Duke said. He tried to sound disapproving, but a fierce and eager light had come into his hooded eyes.

'Not rebellion but reform,' the other man said. 'And justice too! All right-thinking men are aware that English kings have a stronger claim to France than the Valois, but Richard has meekly handed his claim back and taken a daughter of the Valois as his bride, though she is so young he would have done better to adopt her!'

'You intend invasion then.' The Duke frowned. 'Richard Plantagenet is close kin to me. My second wife was his half-sister.'

'And you were trained in the arts of war and the graces of chivalry in my grandfather's Court,' Bolingbroke reminded him. 'You and my father bore arms together in Spain. He too was loyal to Richard, but I know it cost him dear.'

'We are a poor country.' The Duke sucked in his lower lip thoughtfully. 'We have had civil strife here in the past. Even were it not so, I am kin to Richard and have sworn fealty to the Valois.'

'I have asked only for a few nights' shelter,' the other said.

'But you expected more.' The old Duke's glance was sharp. 'I must ponder this, for I'd not break my word to the Valois lightly.'

'Your hospitality suffices me.' The Earl had finished his meal and the smile he sent in Joanna's direction was unexpectedly boyish. 'My stomach was cleaving to my backbone,' he said, 'but now I feel a new man.'

'And a tired man if you've ridden from Paris.' She returned the smile. 'The guest-room is small and seldom used, but I hope you will find it adequate.'

'Until tomorrow then.' He rose and bowed, his smile again including her in a way that made Joanna feel that he saw her as a separate person, not a mere appendage of the Duke.

'He means to topple Richard and seize the throne,' John said when the visitor had retired.

'You think him so ambitious?' she asked cautiously.

'I know him so.' He gave her a fierce nod, mingled with a certain satisfaction. 'He has craved the throne for years. His father's death gives him the opportunity, for he'd not make his move while Gaunt lived. It is a temptation, Joanna, but I would be forsworn and I am too near the end of my life to risk damnation.'

'You must do as you think best,' she answered calmly.

'He's an ambitious man — rich too.' The Duke cupped his chin in his hand. 'His father was content to be a power behind the throne, but Henry Bolingbroke will not be content until he sits on the throne.'

'He is rich?' She spread her hands to the fire.

'Gaunt amassed a fortune and was generous with his children, and Mary de Bohun was the wealthiest girl in England. Henry of Bolingbroke is *very* rich, my dear, though his riches avail him nothing in exile. He will need any help he can obtain if he's to raise a sufficient force to land in England.'

'You must do as you think best,' she said again.

It would be interesting to see the Earl by daylight, she thought, as she prepared for bed. He was not much taller than herself, but his travelling garb had given an impression of bulkiness, and his hands in the firelight had been square and strong. And he was rich, very rich.

Morning brought a quickening of spring. She put on a thinner gown of green silk, belted at the hips with coral, and teased a few strands of hair from her tightly looped plaits to soften her brow. She had always had a high forehead, a sign of intellect her father had told her, but she fancied it was apt to overshadow the rest of her small, neat features. Her figure was still good though a trifle plump, and her skin was rosy. It was as well that Marguerite had been her last child, she decided, pinning a small brooch to her veil. There had been small need recently to dose herself with the remedies prescribed by her father. John was admitting his years at last and seldom came to her bed.

She had no opportunity of speaking privately with the Earl either that day or the next, but she was in no frantic hurry. She was aware that his eyes occasionally strayed towards her as she sat among her ladies and, when she was fairly certain he was not looking at her, she was able to observe him from beneath her lashes. His hair, which had seemed reddish in the firelight, was a deeper brown than she had at first supposed. He wore a short square beard which jutted aggressively when he stood with jaw out-thrust, and even stripped of travelling cape his frame was broad and muscular. She noticed that, though he deferred to his host, he had a set to his lips that told of obstinacy.

She would have liked to join in the conversation but had the wisdom to hold aloof.

Not until the third day, when she mounted the battlements for her evening stroll, did she sight her quarry. He too had ascended the leads and was pacing there, his head bent.

'My Lord Bolingbroke.' She went forward, allowing her cloak to part a little to reveal the green silk beneath. 'Are you fancying yourself neglected or do you come here to escape company?'

'I was thinking of my father,' he said briefly.

'You must think it strange that we do not wear mourning for him,' she said, 'but the truth is that it frets the Duke to be reminded of death. It pants at his own heels.'

'Outward show is not everything.' He spoke mildly.

'John loved your father,' she said. 'It grieves him that he cannot help you in your present plight.'

'He could if he would.' There was a dull resentment in his voice. 'He has ships and men, and I could give them firm promise of payment if he would give them leave to come with me.'

'He is pledged to France and fond of Richard,' she said.

'Before God, madam, but I am fond of Richard myself!' he said explosively. 'One cannot help it, for when he chooses he has a great charm and kindliness, but he is not fit to rule a fleapit. The Londoners hate him and would rise against him at a word. He is arrogant and high-tempered, railing with a womanish fury if any dare cross his will — and his will is never the same from one day to the next!'

'It is said the little Queen loves him well,' Joanna commented.

'Isabella is a child! Of course she loves him when he fusses and pets her and loads her with expensive gifts! He hangs so many jewels upon her it is a wonder she doesn't sink under their weight! But he will beget no child upon her even when she is grown. He cannot love any woman in the way of a true man.'

Isabella de Valois. Joanna repeated the name in her mind. The favoured child of doting parents, the spoiled baby wife of a man who would never condemn her, unthinkingly, to year after year of childbearing.

'My own daughter, Marie, is at the

Court of France,' she said aloud.

'I saw her there, Madam. A pretty girl, and d'Alençon loves her. I wish she had been reserved for my Harry though. He is twelve now, but tall enough to pass for fourteen — or was, the last time I saw him.' He finished speaking abruptly and she saw his jaw clench.

'It is very sad for you to be separated from your family,' she said warmly.

'They are all that remains to me of my beloved Mary.' He spoke quietly, his face shadowed by the dusk. 'You know, my lady, there are many who believe I wed her for the sake of her great wealth, and I'm not denying that it has been useful. Money is always useful. But the truth is that we were boy and girl together and, though my uncle of Gloucester married her older sister and tried to coax Mary into a convent, she would have none of such schemes. She was a sweet maiden and I miss her still.'

'If you were to invade England,'

Joanna said slowly, 'you would depose Richard, would you not?'

'I would prevail upon him to relinquish the throne,' he nodded.

'And take the crown yourself?'

'I would not,' he said, with a sudden flash of humour, 'bestow it upon anybody else.'

'And when you were King you would need a Queen, lest men whispered you were like your cousin?'

'Not to breed heirs.' The amusement was gone. 'My Harry is fit to be king after me, and if, God forbid!, anything were to prevent him, there are Thomas, John and Humphrey to follow him. I'd not give him a rival.'

'It is a very natural sentiment,' she murmured. 'I feel about my own children much as you feel about yours. Fortunately my own childbearing days are done.'

'Surely not!' he said in surprise.

'Not in years,' she agreed, 'but after my last babe, I was assured there would be no more. Marguerite is four years old and still the youngest, so it looks as if my physicians were right. My womb is barren now. It is well, for the Duke is old, and I am nervous when I look into the future. Brittany may be small and impoverished, but its dukedom is an ancient and honourable one, and Jean-Pierre is only eleven.'

'My lady, if ever I sit upon the throne of England, you and yours will enjoy my full protection,' he said earnestly.

'To hear you say so eases my mind somewhat. The Duke — ' She paused.

'My lady?'

'Oh, it is only that I do have a little influence with the Duke. If I were to tell him of your promise of protection after he was gone he might be disposed to aid you now. Of course he cannot openly flout his allegiance to the Valois king or revoke his kinship with Richard, but he has men and ships — and his old comradeship with your lord father might tip the balance.'

'You would speak for me? I have

argued so far to no avail, and I am reluctant to beg.'

'I will catch him at the right moment,' she promised. 'A wife is more likely to know when that is!'

'Aye, that's true.' His unexpectedly boyish grin flashed out. 'I never underestimate the power of a woman.'

'Alas! as we have not the strength of men we must use our poor wits,' she said.

'But I have heard you are a most learned lady who reads and writes and figures in her head.'

'Household accounts, my lord! But it's true I like to read and write. You know, my married life has been spent here at Vannes and, though I love my home, I sometimes think I would go a little crazy, were it not for my books and the occasional letter that brings me news from the outside world.'

'When I am in England I will write to you,' he said abruptly.

'With news of battles and truces? I

hear sufficient of that from John,' she said wryly.

'I will describe some of the beauties of England,' he said, taking her arm as they prepared to descend the stairs. 'There are many of them, believe me. We have forests still so thick that you could lose yourself in them for a year and a day, but further north there are stretches of moorland where heather grows in great, purple swathes clinging to bare rock beneath. At Avebury we have a circle of standing stones that has been there since before Arthur's time, and — I'm sorry. You must find this tedious.'

For she had stiffened beneath his hand, catching her breath in what he mistook for a suppressed yawn.

'It is not in the least tedious,' she said brightly. 'We have standing stones like the ones you mention at Carnac too. I have, for one reason or another, never visited them.'

'One day you will visit England,' he said firmly.

'After you are King?'

It was his turn to stiffen slightly. Men, Joanna thought, never enjoyed having their darkest ambitions revealed in the light.

'Richard must be taken into protective custody,' he said.

'Against whom are you protecting him?' she enquired.

'Against his own worst excesses. I intend him no harm. He is my cousin, nearly of an age with me though we never had much in common.'

'That I can well imagine,' she said dryly, and went forward into the hall, gliding ahead of him with a picture of herself, graceful and fair, colouring the surface of her mind.

After supper there being no music out of respect for John of Gaunt's death, the company disbanded early. The Duke, grunting with the pain of his swollen joints, leaned upon the shoulder of his squire with a heaviness he would not have revealed a few months before. Time was running out for him, she thought, and felt a pang of something that was as much anger as sadness. He had been a brave warrior and a kindly husband, and it seemed wrong that he should end up sitting in a corner telling over and over the exploits of his youth.

He came to her bedchamber — from habit and because he wanted to talk, she guessed. It had been a long time since he had felt any desire to make love to her. She dismissed her ladies and unbraided her hair, knowing he liked to see it loose and flowing, its gold only lightly streaked with silver.

'You look well tonight, Joanna. Company suits you,' he said.

It was a long time, she reflected, since a few words in an evil man's letter had set him to commit murder.

'The Earl was telling me about England,' she said. 'He loves the land very much.'

'As he should, since he aspires to be king of it,' the Duke said, chuckling at his own wit.

'As to that.' Joanna took up her wide-toothed ivory comb and began to slide it gently down the long length of her hair. 'As to that, my lord, I have been thinking — '

6

She looked fair and frail in black, her face very pale after the long hours she had spent at John's bedside.

'Though it will avail nothing,' the physician had told her. 'The Duke is in his seventies and this combination of ague and rheum would be dangerous for a man half his age.'

But she had insisted on remaining. John had been a good husband despite his faults and failings, and she owed it to him to remain at his side, to assure him by her constant presence that she was still his loving wife. She was also honest enough to admit to herself that her motives had not been unmixed. Once she was a widow she and her children would be in a difficult position unless she could coax John to bequeath her the regency of his Duchy during the minority of Jean-Pierre. At eleven their eldest son was too little to rule and might find himself held hostage by one warring faction or another.

It had not been difficult to put into her husband's head that she was the one best fitted to rule. Throughout their marriage she had managed domestic affairs with thrift and good sense and he had told her more than once that her views on foreign policy were sound. Even his jealousy of Oliver de Clisson could be turned to good account since it was easy to persuade him that De Clisson might seize power once he was dead.

At the last, moved by her soft entreaties, he had sent for his notary and added a codicil to his Will granting her the regency and the custody of their children, and four days later his harsh breathing had changed to a rattle and then to silence.

She was surprised and rather pleased to discover that she missed him very much indeed. They had been wed for fourteen years and, though she had never been in love with him, she had been deeply fond of him. He had always treated her kindly, she reflected. Even his plot against De Clisson's life had sprung out of a flattering jealousy. Of course his harping on long-fought battles had been tedious and he had never given her sufficient money, but all in all it had not been a bad marriage. She owed it to his memory to keep the realm strong and united.

'And I can only do that,' she thought, tapping her fingers on the ledge of the window, 'by bringing Oliver De Clisson within bounds.'

With that end in view she had chosen to wear a gown of black silk, cut more closely to the outline of her figure than most mourning garments, and covered her head with a fine black veil which lay like dark cobwebs over her fair hair. She was still comely, she thought, and her recent loss of weight coupled with the faint shadows of tiredness beneath her eyes gave her a touching and vulnerable air.

She had not summoned Sir Oliver to attend her but sent a polite invitation to which he had returned an equally polite acceptance.

It had been a dismal Yuletide with John recently buried and the lawyers coming every day to explain financial affairs. Too much revenue had been squandered on senseless campaigns that brought no lasting benefit, too many tithes and rents allowed to lapse. Joanna had always had an excellent head for figures, but it was still wearisome to have to sit for hours balancing one account against another, making lists of debts due. She had worked hard, asking questions, checking the answers and, by the time January was rung in, she had an accurate grasp of the affairs of the Duchy.

Now she must bring about formal reconciliation with Sir Oliver and she trusted the method she had chosen was the right one. It was a long time since they had met but it was his admiration for her that had begun the quarrel.

Riders were approaching along the shoreline. She gave a final twitch to her veil and went slowly down the stairs to take up the welcome cup, and order the main door to be opened.

'Your Grace.' He dismounted and came to greet her and, for an instant, she allowed herself to feel like a girl again being greeted by him when she had first come into Brittany to be married to the Duke. It was an illusion that not even her fancy could sustain. Sir Oliver had not been a youngling when they had first met and now he must be well into his fifties and looking it, his hairline receding, his cheeks furrowed.

'It was very good of you to come, Sir Oliver.' Handing him the goblet of welcome she let her fingers brush casually against his and was amused to see that he flushed slightly. Evidently her mirror had not lied.

'My condolences on the death of your late lord,' he said stiffly.

'To me he was always a good lord,'

she said, 'but I fear he was not so to you.'

'He sought my life for a fancied wrong,' Sir Oliver said bluntly. 'It was only by the grace of God that I was not murdered where I lay and afterwards, though he knew me to be innocent, he deprived me of lands and title.'

'And you resent it still. I cannot blame you, but John is dead now. Will you carry on the feud against his children?'

She spoke sadly, eyes veiled by their lashes, as they went into the winter solar where she had so often sat, listening to John prosing about his youthful triumphs, while she plied her needle and suppressed her yawns.

'My daughter would have me remove your children by force and seize the Duchy for myself,' he told her.

'You are reckless to come with only a few companions and admit this,' she said.

But there would be other men strung

out along the road waiting his safe return.

'My daughter is a vengeful and ambitious woman. I refused her demand. God forbid I should sink to the killing of children.'

'Knowing you from the old days,' she answered, 'I could not imagine your ever consenting to such a deed.'

'We were ever good friends, you and I.' He gave her a warmer glance. 'If your father had not poisoned the Duke's mind with his foul insinuations, none of this would have happened.'

'I sometimes think,' she said lightly, seating herself, 'that it is a pity you and I did not bed together, since you were accused of it anyway.'

'Oh, there was a time when I was tempted to look at you with desire,' he said, 'but I would never have placed horns on my liege lord, and thank God it was never more than a passing fancy.'

'Oh.' Her voice was suddenly flat and dull.

'But your father's mischief twisted the Duke's thinking,' Sir Oliver was continuing, oblivious to her reaction. 'To tell you plainly I am as weary of the quarrel as you must be. That was why I came today, to put an end to a feud for which there was never reason.'

'But there was reason,' she thought wistfully. 'John knew, deep within himself, that I would have gone to you if you had beckoned.'

'Then we will put an end to it?' she said aloud. 'You will recognise my regency and pay fealty to my son as his true vassal?'

'And the lands stolen from me by the late Duke will be restored?'

'At once,' she said promptly.

'Those lands yielded rents which the Duke put into his own coffers. Will there be restitution?'

'Alas!' Joanna spread her hands. 'John's affairs are in a sad state, and I have little head for business. It will take many months to untangle the accounts and discover exactly when and how the moneys were spent. Not on me, I assure you. John gave me only a small allowance on which I was expected to perform miracles. Cannot the question of restitution be postponed?'

'I suppose so.' He gave her a faintly wry grin. 'I have no wish to add to your difficulties.'

'My first concern is for my children,' she told him. 'Jean-Pierre, when he is of an age to rule, must rule a land free from strife and internal dissension. If you will kiss my son's hands the other knights and lords will follow. We may then work all together for prosperity. But there is our old friendship that also moves me to this. I would not be at odds with you for any reason.'

'My quarrel was never with you, Lady.' He rose from the stool to which she had gestured him and bowed.

He had grown heavier, she noticed, and his movements were more ponderous. Yet she was so full of remembered tenderness for him that her eyes filled will tears.

'There's no need to weep!' Sir Oliver looked slightly alarmed. 'A reconciliation is a time for smiling, and I have promised that I will not press for restitution until the late Duke's affairs are in order.'

As if she never thought about anything else but money! Joanna's tears were dried up at source and she bit back an impatient retort, saying meekly, 'I will summon my household to witness the fealty-taking.'

The chaplain and lawyers would be there too, lest there be any questions later. The days when she had been trusting had long since passed. Sometimes she wondered if there had ever been a time when she had trusted without reservation or if her father's training had taken root in her nature too early.

Jean-Pierre, summoned from his lessons to sit in the great carved chair that stood upon the dais, looked touchingly young in his tunic and hose of black velvet. He missed his father very much for his father had had a fund of interesting stories about the campaigns he had ridden on and the battles he had fought. However now that he was Duke he must behave like one. His lady mother had impressed that upon him. He had hoped that it meant he could ride out on a campaign, but to his disappointment it merely meant longer lessons, and occasional ceremonies in chapel or hall when he was supposed to sit still and not fidget. At least on such occasions he was allowed to wear the collar of diamonds which had been his father's and the ceremonial dagger in its silver scabbard.

'My lord Duke.' Joanna addressed her son formally, sinking to one knee with as much respect as if she had not threatened him with a spanking the previous day. 'Sir Oliver de Clisson has come of his own will to swear allegiance. Are you willing to accept his fealty?'

'I thought Sir Oliver was a rebel,' Jean-Pierre said in bewilderment.

'The quarrel is made up,' Joanna said, looking vexed. 'Sir Oliver wishes to be reconciled, if it be your will.'

It was obvious what the answer was expected to be. Jean-Pierre wondered what would happen if he refused, then — catching his mother's eye — prudently abandoned the notion. He was not very clear as to why there had been a quarrel in the first place anyway, and the man bowing before him had a pleasant expression though he looked far too old to be a rebel.

'It will be my will,' Jean-Pierre said loudly and the elderly gentleman knelt before him and began the ancient oath.

'With Sir Oliver pacified the other lords will swear fealty too,' Joanna thought. 'I would like to get my hands on his daughter for trying to put murder in his mind. What kind of female advocates the slaughter of children? God grant she spoke in temper without real meaning!'

'And thereto plight thee my troth,' Sir Oliver finished, and kissed Jean-Pierre's hands.

'That was very well done, my lord,' Joanna said approvingly.

There was a spattering of applause from the watching bystanders. Jean-Pierre remembered in time not to join in but his eyes were dancing. Being the Duke of Brittany was not so very hard after all. He had also missed a Latin lesson which pleased him greatly.

Servants were bringing in trays with comfits and goblets of wine. Joanna, signalling to a tutor to escort the Duke away, found Sir Oliver at her elbow.

'You have a fine boy, Lady.' He lifted his goblet to her.

'I have four fine boys,' she returned, 'and as Regent I will do everything in my power to secure their future.'

'You are a good mother, Joanna.' He spoke in less formal fashion. 'A good mother and a good wife. I congratulate you.'

'You know,' she confided impulsively,

'there are times when I find it hard to believe the years have fled by so quickly. I still feel myself to be the girl in the garden. You remember?' Her eyes were fixed upon his face.

'Garden? Ah, yes, of course,' he said, but she knew that he had no idea of what she was talking about. For him the kiss she had treasured through the years had meant nothing at all. It was as painful as having icy water tipped down her back. She caught her breath with the shock of it, and was surprised to hear her own voice saying calmly,

'I am expecting word of doings in England soon. It was a comfort to John that Henry of Lancaster was crowned King before he died.'

'He supported Lancaster's invasion, did he not?'

'Someone had to help Gaunt's son. What manner of king takes a child of eleven to wife, dismisses his chief ministers, and hangs jewels on his lap-dog?'

'Richard Plantagenet set no high

example,' Sir Oliver agreed. 'Yet he has support still, even though he yielded his throne. They say his little Queen makes her servants wear the badge of the white hart, and refuses to have anything to do with Lancas — with King Henry's son. It was hoped to make an alliance there but the little maid will have none of him.'

'I remember how jealous my own daughter was when she heard the little Queen slept in a bed shaped like a swan,' Joanna said. 'Well, swan or whatever, 'tis certain Richard would never have shared it with her. Now he is caged at Pontefract and she sulks at Windsor, demanding to be sent home!'

'Is your daughter happy in France?' he asked.

'Very content. Her husband is enamoured of her and showers her with presents. She is more French then Breton now! She threatens to make me a grandmother soon.'

That was his cue, to protest that she

looked too young for such a role.

'Grandchildren are a great joy,' he said, and more cold water trickled down her back.

She was a fool, she thought bitterly, to try to turn back the clock. Time neither stood still nor marched backwards, and romance was only for the young if it existed at all.

After the departure of Sir Oliver she went to her chamber to change into a warmer gown. The silk had not really achieved what she had hoped it might. The reconciliation had been a public and political one after all.

Wrapped in a fur-trimmed robe she sat by the fire, listening to the draught whistling down the chimneys. Moaning for lost opportunities, she thought wryly, and then shook her head impatiently. As Regent it was her duty to concentrate on the safety and prosperity of her son's person and realm. The other knights would follow Sir Oliver now and swear fealty. Her agents would collect the rents regularly and she would invest the money wisely. Dear God! but she was sick of being penned in this draughty little castle, trying to make ends meet.

A few days later, standing at the same window, she saw the messengers she had sent to England, riding back over the icy drawbridge.

She had sent Yuletide greetings to the new King, the 'usurper' King as many in Europe called him. But Duke John had aided him with men and money when he had made his bid to seize his cousin's throne, and he had answered her message with one of his own, sealed in a small packet.

'Which His Grace of England said I must hand to you personally, Lady,' the man said, on his knee before her.

'The King is well?'

'In excellent health, Madam. We were hospitably received and generously entertained.'

'And his kingdom is at rest?'

'There is disaffection still among the supporters of King Richard — that is

133

Richard of Bordeaux. In Wales the Marcher lords threaten rebellion. But King Henry has strong support from Parliament and a will of his own to put down opposition.'

Joanna thanked the man and dismissed him before opening the packet in the privacy of her chamber.

The letter was longer than she had expected and after the first formal salutations so astonishing in its contents that she read avidly.

'The recent death of your good lord, who was so generous a friend to me in my hour of need, saddened me as much for my own sake as for yours. That he should leave the regency in your hands is proof to me of his good sense as well as his great love for you. I believe that it was through your good offices that Duke John gave me the aid and encouragement that helped me to the throne. I shall ever be grateful for that and, in his honour, do all in my power to aid, comfort and befriend his widow and children.

'Madam, I will go further and risk offending you by referring to a matter which ought not to be addressed to one so recently bereaved. I do so only because, as a royal widow, your hand will soon be sought by many princes. I have never forgotten your kindness and courtesy to me, nor do I believe that your hospitable kindness was feigned. For that reason I make bold now to ask you not to rush into any new marriage when your time of mourning is up. I wish you to consider these facts. Brittany is a small land requiring the protection of a larger one against the powerful states surrounding it. The ties between our countries have ever been close. An alliance between us would be of benefit to both.

'My marriage was, like yours, a happy one and my wife's death a great grief to me. She gave me children whom, I hope, you would learn to love as your own and I, for my part, would be good father to your children. These factors ought to be weighed in the balance as should the inescapable truth that neither man nor woman was created to live alone.

'When I met you I was struck by the circumstance that a lady so endowed with comeliness and wit should be a mere duchess, and I resolved then that should the occasion present itself I would offer more.

'Forgive these rude words for they come from the heart of one who has ever been your admirer.'

Joanna's plucked brows could not rise any higher. The new King of England trampled down conventions with as little regard for the proprieties as he had driven a kingly cousin from his throne. 'Mere duchess' indeed! She was not sure she wished such a patronising tone from a man two years her junior. But a handsome man. Her lips quirked as she recalled his well knit figure and thick reddish brown hair. Such a man might prove interesting, but it was too soon. It was far too soon even to think of such matters. He still had his kingdom to subdue and she had her husband to mourn.

There was an enclosure, wrapped in velvet. She untied the ribbon that held it and lifted out a jewel. A forget-me-not, fashioned of turquoise on a golden pin. There was no written message, but it needed none. She laid letter and jewel away, the smile still on her lips. Were she to become Queen of England there would be many such jewels waiting for her in the future.

7

'My dear Joanna, you cannot possibly be serious,' her uncle of Burgundy had said.

'Perfectly serious. King Henry and I were betrothed by proxy three months ago.' She had spoken solemnly though the expression on her uncle's face made her want to giggle.

'Without consulting your relatives? Without asking the advice of your confessor?'

'I don't need anyone's permission to take another husband,' she said flippantly.

'John of Brittany — '

'Has been dead for upward of two years. He was a good man and we lived happily together, but he would be the last one to expect me to live alone for the rest of my life.'

'But to Henry Bolingbroke!'

'King Henry the Fourth,' she said briskly. 'Perhaps you forget that Richard was deposed.'

'And most foully murdered in Pontefract by that same man you are calmly proposing to wed.'

'He was killed by unknown assailants.'

'I was not suggesting,' her uncle said, 'that Henry strangled him with his own hands!'

'And nobody has said that he was strangled,' she snapped. 'There are those who say he deliberately starved himself to death.'

'And those who distribute silver harts as a token that he still lives. I know that too. Joanna, you cannot have thought everything out clearly! Henry has his eye on the throne of France as well as England and will use his marriage with you to gain a foothold in Brittany for the landing of his troops. I'm sorry to sound unkind, my dear, but in wedding you he furthers his French claims!'

'Perhaps. I take no interest in politics,' she said indifferently.

'It is not as if he needs an heir. He had a large family by Mary de Bohun.'

'And I have a family of my own.'

'Which brings me to my most pressing anxiety.' He leaned forward. 'Your eldest son is now Duke of Brittany and must swear his allegiance to Charles de Valois. There can be no question of his going to England with you.'

'He is only fourteen!'

'An age when most lads have already cut the apron strings. He is too old to be in his mother's care and too young to assume full responsibility over his inheritance. In England he would be the king's stepson, bending the knee to the king's son.' Burgundy paused, aware of her strained attention. 'Would you have any of your boys in that situation?'

'What would you have me do?' she said at last.

'Appoint me as guardian to him and your other sons. I was your mother's brother, my dear, and I care for you and yours as if you were all my own. Let them remain here or come with me into France. Their sister is already there and happy with d'Alençon.'

She bit her lip, considering.

'The Breton lords have always been a quarrelsome crew, as your late husband knew,' he urged. 'It will be hard to keep them in check now that they are ruled by a young boy. It will be impossible if that boy is absent in England.'

He was talking sense and she trusted him, but the decision was a painful one. She rose abruptly and went over to the window, staring out into the sunlit courtyard. Jean-Pierre was there, coaching his brothers in the use of the lance and battle-axe. He had shot up since his father's death, seeming now to be all legs and arms, but he would be a handsome man before long. Even now he had the gift of making others respond to his will. The three younger boys were leaping and feinting to his instructions, though Jules had clearly begun to drag his feet.

'Jules is not as strong as the rest,' she said unsteadily. 'He — he takes cold easily, and Richard — he is having trouble with his back teeth. They grow crooked in the gum and pain him when he chews.'

'I will take good heed to their wants,' her uncle said.

'And in the French Court? How will they fare there? Charles is mad, they say, and Queen Isabeau amuses herself with many lovers.'

'The King has periods of lucidity,' he said heavily, 'and the Queen — who can blame her if she forgets her troubles by flinging herself into every extravagance and pleasure? You know she has another daughter now?'

'I heard — Katherine, is it not?'

'The queen takes no interest in the babe, nor in her sisters. They are cared for by servants whose wages, as often as not, remain unpaid. I am sorry for them.'

'Their big sister, Isabella, did well enough,' Joanna said with a flash of spite.

'Her marriage to Richard, you mean? Aye, poor soul, he won her heart with his loving kindness.'

'Not to mention a swan-shaped bed.' She tapped her fingers along the sill.

'Well, Bolingbroke — *King* Henry kept her jewels and bundled her back to her father's Court. You have more reason to pity than to envy her.'

'I have no reason to envy anyone!' she said sharply. 'Very soon I will be Queen of England.'

'And the boys?' He had joined her at the window and his glance towards them was affectionate.

'I will entrust them to you,' she said. 'It is time they began their knightly training anyway, but Blanche and Marguerite will come with me into England.'

'You will leave a regent in Brittany?'

'Sir Oliver de Clisson.' She saw the disappointment in his face and smiled.

'It is no reflection upon you, uncle. You will have the custody of the Duke, but the affairs of Brittany must be administered by one who lives here and puts the welfare of Brittany first. Sir Oliver made rebellion here once, I know, but that quarrel was settled long since and he is devoted to my interests.'

'He will ensure that the revenues bequeathed to you by your husband are paid?'

'He will do everything that is needful,' she assured him, 'and you need not fret that he might try to seize Brittany for himself. He is loyal.'

Loyal because once, long ago, there was a moment when he might have loved me.

Her uncle of Burgundy had stayed for more than a month and, when he had ridden out, her four sons had gone with him, too excited at the prospect of the new life in France to have any space for regrets. It was right that boys should leave home, Joanna told herself firmly, but their going left her with a dull ache. To distract her mind she took out the most recent of Henry's letters.

'Most dear friend and lady,

'I greet you with the hope that you continue well. My own health and that of my children remains excellent, which pleases me much. I trust that yours are also well and that Jules is outgrowing the delicacy of which you spoke. This summer the plague has been less virulent than formerly for which we all offer thanks.

'Queen Isabella is to return to France and will probably be at her father's Court before this letter reaches you. I had hoped to sway her mind towards marriage with Harry, but she remains obdurate. At fourteen she has the spirit of a grown woman. It is annoying but I cannot avoid a feeling of admiration for a girl who knows her own mind so well. So I must give in with a good grace and find my son another bride. At present he is more interested in making war than love! If the Welsh chieftains continue to oppose me I must undertake an expedition to their barbarous regions. They have always been hot in Richard's cause and even his death, which many of them refuse to believe in, does not induce them to pay fealty to me. I will send Harry against them for though he is only fifteen, he already displays an eagerness to fight and a grasp of military tactics remarkable in one so young!

'I believe that the New Year would be an excellent time at which to wed. By then you will have resolved all your affairs in Brittany and I will have made the arrangements necessary for your comfort. It is my intention, after we are united, to provide for you a separate crowning as a mark of my esteem and favour. I believe that my dear Mary, God rest her soul, would have been happy for both of us. My other children look forward eagerly to your arrival. They have been too long without a mother and join with me in sending their prayers and good wishes.

'Your faithful friend,
'Henry.'

It was a pleasant letter. Pleasant and friendly. She read it through twice and laid it down. It was sheer foolishness at her age to expect any word of love, but there was an emptiness at the core of her because there was none.

The months between the departure of her sons into France and her own departure for England went by slowly. Letters, friendly, amiable letters telling of the campaign in Wales, came from Henry. Her uncle of Burgundy wrote to say that the boys were progressing well at their lessons and that Marie was with child.

'I shall be a grandmother before I am a bride,' she said to her reflection in the mirror, and shook her head in smiling disbelief. Her hair and skin had lost the bloom of youth, but she was still a comely woman and the new fashions — the skirt and trailing sleeves turned back to reveal cloth-of-silver, the headdress towering on its framework of ivory — suited her slender graceful frame. She had bought new clothes with almost reckless abandon, determined that never again would she scrimp and save as she had been forced to do during John's lifetime. She could scarcely wait to arrive in England, but at the last, when she rode out of Vannes, an unexpected sadness tugged at her heart. In this tiny corner of a tiny duchy she had spent half her life, borne her children, known contentment with a man who had been more father than husband. Suddenly it was very hard to leave it all behind.

Less than a month since, after five days tossing in the storm-swept channel, she had landed at Falmouth and fancied for a moment that, by some mischance, she had been thrown back onto the Breton coast, for there was the same grey rock with the little houses huddled against it, the same jagged rocks against which the white-crested waves crashed and broke.

'We were supposed to land at Southampton.' Carried ashore, for there was no decent wharf, Joanna gazed round her blankly.

'There are horses on the way, Your Grace!' One of her escort knights panted up to her. 'Seems the King's waiting at Winchester, but the storm was so bad that he had a watch set at every port lest you land there!'

'Surely I am not expected to continue my journey in these garments?' She frowned down at the wet hem of her trailing skirt.

'Falmouth Castle is only a short ride. I was here before, Your Grace, and remember it very well,' another said. 'They will have food and a night's lodging there, surely!'

'Let us hope so,' she said wryly.

There ought to have been crowds and cheering, not this sorry little procession of travel-stained people, stared at by a few black-browed fisherfolk who had ventured out to see them. Even the horses, when they arrived, looked fitter for pulling a plough than carrying a queen. For a moment she had a strong desire, storm or no storm, to head out to sea again, and then, her sense of humour overcoming her, she found herself laughing.

'Let us to Falmouth Castle,' she said, 'and pray that Englishmen don't object to a raggle-taggle queen!'

That had been an inauspicious start, she thought now, bowing her head as the choir began a Te Deum. However, matters had improved rapidly. There had been lodging and provisions at the castle and by the time fresh and better horses had been secured she felt rested from the ravages of the journey.

They had tarried several days at Falmouth until the official escort arrived, and Joanna had had her first glimpse of the boy Harry. He was taller than his father, his hair black and cropped in the new fashion she privately considered to be ugly, but he had strong features and a quick, decisive manner that made him seem older than fifteen.

'I bid you welcome, Your Grace.' He kissed her hands with a fine show of courtliness. 'You had a rough journey to your new home but I trust we'll make all smooth now.'

'I am happy to have your company,' she said, relieved that he didn't appear to resent her. She had been apprehensive lest affection for his dead mother made him surly.

'Oh, we will see you safely to Winchester and from thence to London, Madam. It is many days' ride so I hope it will not tire you too much.' He shot her a faintly worried glance as if he feared she might crumble into dust before him.

'I will try to keep pace with you,' she said, restraining a smile.

'Oh, I generally ride like the wind,' he said with something of a boy's boastfulness. 'I am just back from campaign, so I am accustomed to long hours in the saddle.'

'In Wales. I heard of it.'

'We chased Owen Glendower back to his mountain lair! It will be a long time before they emerge to stir up trouble for my father by calling him usurper!'

'Do many call him that?'

He shrugged, his young face hardening.

'We pay them no heed. The realm needs good government which my father can provide, and Richard Plantagenet never could.'

'What was he like?' She could not repress her curiosity.

'Richard? To me he was always kindly.' There was reluctance in his voice. Perhaps it troubled his conscience to know that the king who had always been kind to him had been deposed and murdered to smooth his own pathway to the throne.

'And his queen?'

'Isabella?' A warmth had stolen into his voice. 'I intended to marry her, you know, but she would not have me. She would not even speak to me when I called upon her. She mourned for Richard and in the end we had to let her return to France. But we kept her dowry and divided up her jewels. They say now she will marry her cousin of Orléans, so I no longer think of her.'

But it was evident that she had caught his fancy and that his pride had been hurt by her rejection of his suit.

The journey to Winchester had been less arduous than she had feared. They had ridden in easy stages, first through wild and rocky country that reminded her more and more of Brittany and then over a featureless moor, where the only dwelling-places to be seen were occasional rudely-thatched huts. Her escort clustered tightly round her, swords drawn, and she was glad when they left the wilderness behind and came in sight of town walls again. They had been lodged at convents along the way where the hospitality, though plain, had been gracious, but Joanna had sensed a certain hesitation in their welcome. She wondered if loyalty to the memory of King Richard prevented the nuns from offering a more whole-hearted greeting, or if they were shy in the presence of a queen. Although the actual marriage ceremony had not yet been solemnised, she had already been styled as queen. It would be unfortunate, she thought with an inward smile, if Henry changed his mind about wedding her when he saw her again face to face.

Any shadow of apprehension she might have felt was dispersed by his cordial greeting when at last they reached Winchester. He had not altered in the three years since their meeting and she felt shy as a girl when he stepped out from the courtiers surrounding him, put his arms about

154

her, and kissed her full on the mouth,
'So! you are in England at last!' He
put his arm about her, turning her to
face the assembled company. 'Harry
took great care of you, I trust?'

'Most gallant care, sir,' she answered,
smiling.

'He's a fine boy.' Henry sent his heir
a glance of approbation. 'There are my
other lads — Thomas, John, Humphrey
— they're much of an age with your
own. I wish you had brought them
into England instead of giving in to
your uncle of Burgundy's demands.'

'I have my daughters here.' She
indicated Blanche and Marguerite who
hung back shyly.

'They are as welcome as my own
daughters,' Henry said. 'Why, madam,
between us we have already thirteen
younglings! Who can say now that King
Henry has no support in the country?'
He looked round challengingly and
there was laughter, but Joanna detected
an uneasiness behind it. The usurpation
of the crown and the murder of King

Richard still lay uneasily on men's minds. It would be a long time before they forgot.

The marriage had been a sumptuous affair. She had worn cream brocade, thickly sewn with pearls and amethysts, the wide-horned headdress veiled in silver lace. Her own daughters and Henry's two girls, clad in kirtles of pale blue with wreaths of white silk roses about their heads, had attended her, the two fair heads and the two dark heads nodding together as they whispered. At least the princesses had made friends, she thought, and felt a pang for her own absent sons. But it was not the time for sadness. She was marrying Henry of England and the day demanded celebration.

The Te Deum had ended. She glanced up through her lashes and saw Henry still in the shadow of the curtained gallery.

'The day will be yours alone,' he had told her. 'You will have equal rank with me, Joanna.'

There had been a hint of defiance in his tone. She wondered if his Coronation was Henry's way of justifying his choice of wife. Although she had been only a short time in England she was already aware that his marriage had not found universal favour. There were many who would have preferred him to take a young bride instead of a mature widow, and others who felt Brittany was too closely allied to France. And she had heard, in a whisper hastily suppressed, the name of her father — Charles the Bad, noted for his cruelty, his dark moon knowledge.

'Your Grace?' One of the clerics had stepped forward to assist her to her knees. Christianity was all bobbing and bowing, Joanna thought, and hastily fastened her gaze upon the ivory and silver prayerbook laid on the ledge of the prayer stool.

'*Dominus vobiscum et cum spiritu sancto.*' She murmured the words on the right-hand page, but the page fluttered in the draught from the great door and the flyleaf bore writing in a childish scrawl,

'For my dear lord and husband, Richard, from Isabella his Queen.'

8

Being a queen was infinitely better than being a duchess, Joanna reflected with satisfaction, looking round her private parlour with its hangings of woven silk, the Turkish carpet on the stone floor, the stained-glass windows through which sunlight glowed, the carved chests and high-backed chairs of dark oak, the hand mirror and jewel box of ivory, the goblets of Venetian crystal that reflected the leaping flames of the fire which she insisted on having lit even during the summer. There were similar hangings in her bedchamber and in the presses numerous new gowns were laid with sprigs of rosemary against the day when she could choose to wear them. All the rooms were as rich and luxurious in every one of the castles she had seen since her arrival in England. When they moved from one residence to the next the furnishings were packed up and carted ahead, so that when the royal party arrived the bare walls and echoing apartments were ready for occupation.

It was a far cry from the draughty castle of Brittany from where she had looked out during endless winters across bleak shores to the tossing sea. The ivory-backed mirror reflected a charming face surmounted by a jewelled cap beneath which her fair hair was plaited into a golden net. There were more jewels at the neck of her satin gown and the sash girdling her hips was thickly encrusted with gold. That too was a far cry from the mended gowns she had worn as Duchess of Brittany.

There was no need for her to envy the comforts that had once been showered on little Queen Isabella. The child who had been loyal to Richard of Bordeaux and refused to marry the son of the man she had considered to be a usurper had been stripped of her jewels, routed out of her swan-shaped bed, and sent back to her parents. What irritated Joanna slightly was that the obstinate child was still regarded with some regret by the King's son.

'A girl so strong-minded would have proved a good helpmate,' he said.

'An obstinate one,' Joanna corrected.

'Perhaps.' He frowned a little and then darted her a mischievous look. 'But she would have brought me the dowry of France, and my father needs it. The Welsh campaigns cost us a great deal of money, and the Welsh are not yet subdued.'

Joanna was torn between the desire to smile and the desire to yawn. Young Harry was so boyish in his enthusiasm for the girl who had refused to marry him, and so tedious in his endless recitals of the campaign he had been in. It seemed to her that men, whatever their age, spent too much time retelling old battles, in all of which they remembered playing a heroic part. John's repetitions of the Battle of Aurey had stupefied her with boredom. She wondered if it would have been the same with Oliver de Clisson. If anything between them had ever occurred and they had married, would he have declined into an elderly bore? It was a fruitless speculation since she would probably never meet him again. At thirty-four she was past the age when a kiss in a garden would have meant anything at all. Yet the mirror informed her that she was still a comely woman. Childbearing had rounded her tall figure and thanks to the care she took her skin was as clear and soft as a girl's, her hair pale golden. Henry the King certainly appreciated her charms. His love-making was frequent and skilful and, if he praised his dead wife a little too often, Joanna reminded herself that she ought to be pleased. A man who has tender memories of his first mate is likely to treat the second with consideration. And thank the Lord, as he already had a family, he did not expect her to bear him any more children, though she was always careful after he had visited her room to use the douche soaked in the infusion she prepared when the moon was dark. Women, she thought, were entitled to use such stratagems to protect themselves from the burdens of endless childbearing.

This marriage was for her a late flowering. For the first time in her life she had clothes and jewels and leisure in which to enjoy herself. Henry was a cultured man with a fondness for music and dancing, and he was a man who appreciated the charm of a harmonious domestic atmosphere. There were times when she was almost in love with him. Certainly she was fond of his children. Her own sons and Marie were so far away, and Blanche and Marguerite would soon be leaving her in order to be married. Henry's lively, high-spirited brood helped assuage the ache in her heart and she was particularly fond of Harry despite his youthful boasting about the Welsh campaign.

She turned somewhat reluctantly, from the contemplation of her own charms in the mirror and drew out from her sleeve the poem she had found pinned to her pillow the previous evening. It was a very bad poem, full of pleas to a beauteous queen to have mercy and smile on a wretch who adored her from afar. The wretch in question had signed his name with a flourish, and she smiled at the bold Edward of York that adorned the page. The King's cousin was a lively, impetuous courtier who flirted with her shamelessly whenever he got the opportunity. No doubt he was hoping for favours but it was flattering to be admired.

A hand descended over her shoulder, plucking the paper from her.

There were times, Joanna thought, when Henry could move as quietly as a cat. He was frowning, his chin thrust out so that his close-clipped beard had a suddenly aggressive quality.

'How long has my cousin of York

been penning you messages of love-liking?' he enquired.

'It's merely a poem.' She spoke warily, uneasy at the expression on his face.

'How many of these has he written?'

'Only that one, as far as I know. It's very bad.'

'Yet you cherish it sufficiently to hide it in your sleeve?'

'I was intending to show it to you.'

'When did he give it to you?'

'He bribed one of my maids to pin it to my pillow, I suppose. I have not seen Edward in a week.'

'Then why did you not show it to me at once?'

'Because you have been in Council all morning.' Joanna's voice expressed surprise and a dawning resentment. 'Surely you did not expect me to come running to you with it?'

'I like to be informed of my wife's activities,' Henry said.

'*My* activities! It was your cousin who wrote the poem!'

'With your encouragement? In the knowledge that it would please you?'

'Well, I dare say he hoped that it would,' Joanna said and broke off to exclaim, 'Why, you don't object, do you? It is natural for young men to write verse.'

'And pin them to the pillows of married ladies?'

'Oh, Henry, don't be foolish!' she exclaimed. 'It is mere custom, that's all.'

'Some customs are not so admirable,' he said sulkily. 'You are my wife and should be circumspect. Your position here is a delicate one. There were many who murmured against my marrying you.'

'Your own position is also somewhat delicate,' Joanna said sharply. 'There are many who call you usurper and whisper you should never have been crowned.'

To her surprise the sulkiness fled from his face to be replaced by a haunted, brooding look.

'I did what I did out of necessity,' he said slowly. 'You must believe me when I tell you that I had no personal spite against Richard. But he was a bad king, Joanna. Weak and charming and always ready to break a promise! Whoever tried to control his excesses was banished. My father died a broken man, denied permission to meet with me. John of Gaunt was Richard's most loyal uncle, but he too was tossed aside. Richard lost all the lands his father and grandfather had won, and spent his time in being mothered by his first wife and fondling his second. Yet people remember only that the child Queen conceived a passion for him and that his mother was the fair maid of Kent. They remember only that he died — murdered, they say, by me, though there are as many claim he is still alive and will one day be restored to the throne. They paint a portrait of the man they wanted him to be and say he was that man. Dead he is a more formidable enemy than when he was alive! And I am determined to win back for England all the land that my cousin of Bordeaux lost and to hold my throne — *my* throne!'

He paused but it was only to draw breath. His face had reddened and a vein throbbed in his temple. Joanna, staring at him, thought with sudden clarity.

'But he is consumed with guilt over the death of King Richard.'

'The people will learn to respect me.' Henry had resumed his tirade. 'They will learn that a King must be strong and resolute and that his personal life must be above reproach. We will set an example of conjugal fidelity, Joanna. The commons will cease whispering about Richard's handsome presence and his baby wife! They will respect us both, Joanna! And you will not again compromise your reputation by receiving effusions of love from my cousin of York!'

'It scarcely seems — ' Joanna bit her lip, then said equably, 'Of course you are right, Henry. I had not thought that so small a matter could cause any difficulties for you. It was foolish of me.'

'York has been casting sheep's eyes at you since we were wed,' Henry said. 'People are already gossiping about his partiality.'

'Oh, surely not!' Joanna repressed a giggle, seeing the sulkiness back in the King's face, and sensing the dangerous moment had passed. 'My lord, I am not a young and beautiful girl after all. I am middle-aged with seven children and it is mere foolishness on his or anyone else's part to imagine there could be any foundation to the rumours.'

'The rumours can harm you.' Henry was not so easily mollified. 'Joanna, the people loved Isabella of France. She was only a child and never would have been full wife because Richard could never have been full husband, but she was sweet and loyal, and the people took her to their hearts. I want them to take you to their hearts, to cherish you as I cherish you, Joanna.'

It mattered to him that the people should love her because that would make his throne more secure. She must be above reproach, free from the merest hint of scandal. It had nothing to do with personal jealousy.

'I have done nothing to make the people dislike me,' she said stiffly.

'There are complaints,' Henry said.

'What complaints? Who dares complain?' Joanna said, rising indignantly.

'Your servants are all Breton,' he told her. 'The rents from your Breton inheritance go into your own coffers while the wages of your servants come from the Privy Purse. My advisers feel that, if you insist on having foreign servants, you should make offer to pay them out of your own revenues.'

Joanna stared at him, a chill shuddering through her. Surely the King couldn't be serious! As a child she had been told over and over again that no man would marry her save for her dowry because she was the daughter of Charles the Bad. At the Court of France only Oliver de Clisson had ever complimented her. And the long years in Brittany when she had scrimped and saved were too recent to have lost their sting.

'My revenues are small,' she said at last. 'I cannot be expected to pay my own servants!'

'Then you must take English ones and send your Bretons home.'

'They have been loyal to me. Why should I send them back?'

'It is either that or you must pay them out of your own revenues,' he said.

'I will send half of them home,' Joanna said after a long moment. 'But the wages of the rest and of any English servants engaged on my behalf must be paid out of the Privy Purse.'

'Then you must manage with fewer servants,' Henry said.

Joanna took an agitated turn up and down the room. The chill was warming into anger now. All the loving words spoken by the King were worthless if she could not continue to enjoy the luxury in which the first year of her marriage had been spent.

'I would not be a burden,' she said slowly, 'but as Queen I am entitled to maintain a certain state.'

'Naturally, but your household is very large,' Henry said.

'And how large do your advisers feel it should be?' she enquired sweetly.

'You have a cook to prepare the dishes that please your palate.' To her annoyance he pulled a list from his pouch and consulted it. 'My Council feel that you are entitled to retain his services as well as that of your Dame and your Mistress of the Robes. Two knights and two chambermaids would suffice your needs, and two esquires, and a nurse for those days in the month when your flowers come upon you, and a messenger — and various washer-women and seamstresses.'

'But that is no household at all!' she cried. 'How can I keep queenly state with such a paltry retinue?'

'Joanna, when I first met you you wore a patched dress and were helping your maid to prepare supper,' he said.

'And you were banished from England and seeking John of Brittany's help to topple Richard from the throne. I persuaded him to give you that help.'

'And I will always love you for it.' He came across and kissed her hand. 'My dearest Queen, I love you dearly, and I want my people to love you too. Will you accept the changes in your household?'

'If the wages are paid — out of the Privy Purse?' She shot him a challenging glance.

'If you will send the rest of your Bretons back to their home.'

'Yes, of course.' She nodded. 'I will send nearly all of them back to Brittany if it pleases you, but I would beg a favour in return.'

'The payment of the wages?'

'I do not need to beg for what is my right as your Queen,' she said, then softened her tone as she saw the vein jump in his forehead again. 'No, if I send back my servants then you must grant me a small boon.'

'Anything my beloved Queen wants,' he said.

'There are Breton sailors held in Cornwall. I would have them released.'

'They are pirates who attacked our trade boats and were themselves taken prisoner.'

'I would have them freed,' she repeated.

'To do so would anger the Council,' he began, but she interrupted him, her voice low and passionate.

'You told me that the people despised King Richard because he let his Council rule! Will you allow your Council to dictate everything to you? Henry, you are King and I have craved a boon from you. Your meanest subject should be able to rely on your word, my lord King, and I am surely more to you than that! I have agreed to cut down my household, so cannot you keep your promise to me?'

'You keep me to my word most charmingly,' he said, but the frown remained on his face, the beard was still aggressive.

Always it was necessary to stroke men in order that they would not bite. Herself as a child, curtsying to her father, 'Yes, my lord father, I will do as you wish.' Herself as a girl in the French Court, 'Your Highness, it will grieve me so much not to be here in your company.' Herself as a young woman in Brittany, 'Tell me again about the Battle of Aurey, John. I have forgotten how it goes.' An evil King, an insane King, a prosy old Duke — and now there stood the husband she almost loved, who could take away the jewels and the clothes and the pretty rooms where the fires were lit even in the summer.

'I would ask a further favour,' she said. 'It is — to tell truth your cousin of York's open devotion embarrasses me a little. It offends me that he should consider me to be the kind of woman who holds her marriage vows so lightly that she would be flattered by such nonsense. I would teach him a sharp lesson if it were in my power.'

'You cannot expect me to cut off my cousin's head merely because he admires you,' Henry said, smiling now, with the vein no longer throbbing.

'A short imprisonment would do him no harm.'

'Three months for offending my Queen.' Henry looked thoughtful, then nodded. 'He may not admire you so greatly when he comes out.'

'Perhaps he will write better poetry,' Joanna said sharply.

Henry threw back his head and laughed. When he laughed he looked again like the young man who had come into Brittany and talked with John about the weak King Richard.

'Joanna, I chose wisely when I chose you as my Queen!' He drew her to him and kissed her. 'I have been fortunate in both my wives. Now I go to give cousin Edward a fright he will not soon forget!'

When he had strode from the room Joanna sat down abruptly on the stool again. The King had been stroked but until this moment she had not realised it would ever be necessary to do so.

A month later most of her Breton household, together with the Breton pirates captured off the Cornish coast, sailed away. Joanna had hoped that her willingness to comply with the Council's wishes would bear fruit in the form of increased popularity for herself, but the arrest of Edward of York, though it amused the King, had had a contrary effect upon his advisers. Sheltered though she was within her apartments, Joanna sensed a coldness around her.

Henry's new Queen, the whispers ran, had caused the King to release the pirates, had caused the detention of a popular Duke for the most frivolous of causes. Worst of all she was giving the revenues from her Breton estates to her children who, in turn, passed them on to the King of France.

'It is all nonsense,' her eldest stepson told her loftily, 'but people always twist a tale, and you are not in a position to deny openly rumours that run in secret. Of course, if you were to cede your rents — ' He paused, flushing slightly.

'To help your father make war in France?' Joanna shook her head. 'Hal, try to understand. I am eager for England to regain the possessions that King Richard lost, but when I was a girl I lived in France and was most kindly treated. My children, Marie and Arthur, have made French marriages. I cannot allow my paltry little inheritance to be used for either side. I would stand above politics.'

It sounded high-minded and the prince seemed to accept it as such, but to herself she admitted wryly that the reasons she had given him were spurious. Within herself she knew that her inheritance was a shield against an uncertain world where fathers worshipped evil and husbands had to be pampered and even an innocent verse held the possibility of disaster.

9

Joanna, reading the letter, felt as if a voice from the past had called out in well-remembered tones reminding her of herself when young. Sir Oliver de Clisson was asking for the hand of her youngest daughter for his grandson.

'That by virtue of the great amity that has ever existed between us we may join these two in a loving partnership,' the letter ran in his bold, square hand.

Marguerite was twelve and had been at the English Court since her mother's marriage to King Henry. Both she and her sister, Blanche, were fair, gentle children, not clever or fascinating, but, in Joanna's eyes as least, charming in their naïveté. To have the girls near her made up to a small extent for the absence of Marie and her sons, and the King, himself a family man, had encouraged her to keep both her daughters in close attendance. But royal girls were expected to marry and their marriages were affairs of state and had very little to do with the 'loving partnership' of which Oliver Clisson wrote.

'He writes as if he were of equal rank.' Henry frowned slightly as he read the letter she passed to him.

'The De Clissons are an ancient and noble family,' Joanna said defensively, 'and Sir Oliver was close friend to my late husband.'

'He writes as if he had also been close friend to you,' Henry said dryly.

'Oh, when I was a child I thought him the perfect knight,' she said lightly, 'but he is old now and it is years since I laid eyes on him.'

She wondered if the King had ever been told of the Duke's baseless jealousy and of the abortive murder attempt. It seemed that he had not for after a moment he gave the letter back to her, saying mildly,

'They are your daughters, my dear.

You have my consent to bestow them where you please.'

'I will write to Sir Oliver. Perhaps it would be possible for me to attend the wedding.'

'My dear, I could not spare you out of England,' he said. 'As it is the expense of two dowries will be a strain on your resources.'

'My resources! Am I expected to provide the dowries?' Joanna looked at him in consternation.

'You have your Breton rents.'

'The harvest was a meagre one last year. I could not possibly find a dowry for Marguerite,' she said hastily.

'And the Privy Purse is slender. The Welsh continue to bother us and the campaign in France is at stalemate.'

'Richard's first wife,' Joanna said absently.

'Anne of Bohemia. She died of the plague, poor lady,' Henry said. 'My cousin of Bordeaux fired her palace of Shene and watched it burn. He loved her as if she were his mother, I believe, for certainly they never bedded.'

'He burned down an entire palace just because his wife died!' Joanna gasped.

'Out of grief,' Henry said.

'Then he must have been truly mazed in the head! I am not surprised that he couldn't rule his kingdom properly. Did he burn her jewels too?'

'No I believe not.'

'Who wears them now? And her allowance from the Privy Council? I have heard that Richard's first queen had a handsome allowance.'

'It was discontinued after her death, I suppose.' The King had begun to look uncomfortable.

'Surely the Council will not pay less honour to your wife than to Richard's?' Joanna said.

'You want an allowance from the Privy Council?'

'I believe that I am entitled to what Anne of Bohemia enjoyed,' Joanna said primly. 'Out of it I will, of course, pay my daughter's dowry.'

'You are a clever woman, my Joanna.' Henry gave her a smile of somewhat grudging approval. 'I will speak to the Council. For my own part I respect your wishes.'

'You are always good to me, Henry,' she answered. 'But no man,' a small voice whispered, 'will ever set a palace ablaze out of sorrow for your dying.'

The Council, after some argument, agreed to continue the allowance once paid to Anne of Bohemia, and those jewels of the dead queen's that could be traced were duly presented to Joanna. They were beautiful, she thought, as she slid a rope of milky pearls over her wrist and lifted a glittering carbuncle to the light. They were truly beautiful and certainly very valuable. She would bestow some of the pieces upon her daughters as wedding-gifts. Lifting the carbuncle again, watching the colours at its heart change and flash, she wavered a little. Blanche and Marguerite were children and elaborate jewels looked out of place on little girls. For the moment at least she would keep them herself.

Marguerite accepted the news that she was to go to Brittany to be married with the placid docility that was part of her nature. She did not even seem very interested in the boy she was going to wed.

'Alain de Rohan is fifteen and they tell me he is a fine lad,' Joanna said encouragingly.

'Will you sail with us?' Blanche asked. There was a wistful note in her voice.

Henry had finally and reluctantly given her permission to travel to Brittany.

'But it must be at your own expense, Joanna. I cannot go cap in hand to the Council demanding more and more money for you,' he had warned.

To return to Brittany would mean having to spend some of the allowance recently granted to her. It would also mean meeting Sir Oliver again. Better to remember him in his vigour, better for him to keep a picture somewhere in his mind of the girl she had been, better to save the money.

'Lady de Rohan is sailing to England and will take you back with her,' she said aloud. 'Lady Margot is Sir Oliver's daughter and will be good mother to you when you are wedded to her son.'

She was curious about Sir Oliver's daughter who was about her own age. Lady de Rohan was slightly lame as the result of a childhood accident, but when the lady arrived she gave little indication of infirmity save that she leaned on a silver-headed cane.

There was nothing in her to remind Joanna of Sir Oliver. Clearly Margot resembled her mother, Joanna thought, covertly studying the sharp nose, the long eyes under their thick, reddish lashes, the carefully coiled auburn hair.

'But they are both so sweet, Your Grace,' she fluted, drawing the princesses towards her. 'My son will be demanding the right to wed both of them!'

'They are both well bred and

educated according to their station,' Joanna said, and wished that the sentence hadn't come out sounding as if she were asking for approval.

'Sweet things!' The long eyes slid away from her while the high, breathless voice continued. 'My lord father wishes to be remembered to you. He has always had a most affectionate regard for the memory of Duke John. He spent so much time with him that my lady mother became quite jealous.'

Joanna, listening, thought apprehensively, 'But Lady Margot speaks of herself, not her mother. She has been told at some time or other of the occasion when Duke John ordered her father's murder because of his suspicions about Sir Oliver and me.'

'My daughters have never been away from me,' she said aloud. 'It is hard for me to let them go.'

'Oh, but returning to Brittany will be going home for them,' Lady Margot fluted. 'I shall take good care of both of them, never fear, Your Grace.'

187

It must have been the reflection of the flames on the hearth over her face that made her look for an instant as if, beneath the smile, another expression flickered, watchful and sly. Joanna looked away, unwilling to find what she hoped was only in her imagination.

The next day she stood, resplendent in pale brocade, her eyelids carefully shaded with blue, and watched her two daughters ride away, very erect and grown-up on their ponies, with Lady Margot de Rohan riding between them, her veil floating behind her, the long eyes modestly lowered. There was no fire to cast a deceiving reflection but the corners of her mouth under the sharp nose were slyly tilted.

For a moment Joanna experienced a wild desire to call them back, to declare the journey must be postponed because she had changed her mind and decided to accompany them after all. She did nothing, of course, but stood motionless until the childish figures had trotted out of view and the long train of attendants filled her vision.

A month later she stood, equally motionless, while a perspiring messenger bent his knee and stammered out his message, a message that turned her to stone. It was the King who barked out questions and finally dismissed the man with a handful of silver. Joanna could neither move nor speak. She could only stand with the words the man had spoken beating in her brain.

'The Lady Marguerite was taken ill at the wedding breakfast, complaining of dizziness and stomach pains. A physician was summoned and every possible remedy administered but the princess died at nightfall, and within the hour the Lady Blanche was also stricken and died before the sun rose.'

There was a letter from Sir Oliver de Clisson, hastily written. Henry put it into her hands and, after a long time, she opened it and read the trembling hand that betrayed the shock and grief of the writer.

'There are no words, Your Grace, with which I can express the anguish I feel at the deaths of your two fair children. My grandson is overwhelmed by the loss of his bride for whom he had already conceived a great fondness. For myself I can only say that it has been like losing my own flesh and blood. It is believed that both the princesses succumbed to a sudden fever that attacks in the summer without warning, but you may rest assured that everything possible was done to save them. My grief is as deep as your own, and I join with you in your mourning.'

'He does not mention his daughter's feelings,' Joanna said at last. Her throat hurt when she spoke and her eyes ached with unshed tears.

'My dear — ' The King looked at her, helpless to comfort. She had never seemed colder or more remote, her face white as wax.

'They were poisoned,' Joanna said. 'I am certain they were poisoned.'

'That is nonsense!' Henry exploded, seeking relief in temper. 'Who would poison two innocent children and one of them a bride on her wedding day? This marriage was sought by the De Clissons. There is no reason in the world for anyone to have hurt them!'

No reason save that his daughter believes her father once loved me and so neglected his wife, and she has taken revenge on me through my children. But I can say nothing, prove nothing without setting in motion rumours that were false nearly twenty years ago.

'Will you write to Sir Oliver?' she asked. 'And the — arrangements. You will see to those? Send your instructions?'

'Of course. Full Court mourning for three months.'

'I will go to my room to pray,' Joanna said stiffly and went from the room evading the King's hand. 'If anyone touches me I will break into a thousand pieces. My daughters are dead, and it's my fault because when

191

I was young and foolish I caused an old husband to be jealous, not knowing what I did, not even doing anything a hundred people couldn't have watched. Because of my foolishness my daughters are both dead, dead, dead.'

She opened the carved chest in which her jewels were laid on velvet-lined trays that slid out so that she could choose which pieces to wear for any occasion. There were many precious stones glinting in their settings of gold and silver. Their colours and their shapes were comforting. She lifted a pendant that glittered like white fire. She had meant to give it to Marguerite when the child was older. For a moment she let a single tear roll down her cheek and stain the velvet.

'My lady mother?' She had not heard the Prince enter and, for a moment, she stared at him as if he were a stranger.

At twenty he was a handsome boy, with darker hair and eyes than his father and a more slender build. He had welcomed her pleasantly when she had married the King, and treated her when they met with an affectionate courtesy, but he had never addressed her by any title less formal than 'Your Grace'.

'The King told me about the loss of my sisters.' He came across the room and stood, his head bent slightly, his young features grave.

'Both dead,' Joanna said, and began suddenly to cry without restraint.

'Lady mother,' was all that he said, but his arms were about her and within his boy's protection her own sorrow found expression.

Princesses died. Princesses were married. The three months' mourning being over, Henry's daughters by his first wife were sent away to be married, and the King returned to his campaigning, taking his four sons with him.

'While I sit and spin and fret because no letters come,' Joanna said restlessly.

'You cannot possibly come on campaign,' Henry said genially.

'Other queens have,' she said eagerly. 'Eleanora of Aquitaine rode on Crusade and King Edward the First took his wife of Castille with him to war.'

'Eleanora of Aquitaine led her husband round by the nose,' Henry said, 'and Edward — ' He broke off, then resumed. 'Edward was a law unto himself.'

But he had been going to say that Edward loved his wife, Joanna thought. She was not loved, perhaps had never been. Both her husbands had given her affection, but never the passionate relationship for which her heart craved. Perhaps such relationships did not really exist, she thought sadly.

'Why not go to Langley?' Henry said, a coaxing note in his voice. 'At Langley you can rest and relax.'

As if I were elderly, Joanna thought crossly, whereas I am not yet forty. On the other hand it would be pleasant to winter at Langley. It was one of the most charming of royal palaces, surrounded by woodland and far from the noise and stench of the city. She had begun to dislike the city with its jangling bells, its jostling crowds who unaccountably fell silent when her litter was borne past.

'It is not your fault,' Henry had consoled when she asked the reason. 'The people are stubborn in their loyalties. They weep still for Richard and they remember his Queens.'

'Neither of whom he ever bedded!' Joanna snapped. There were times when she felt as if her entire life had been overshadowed by the examples of other women. Her father had told her once that her mother had been supremely beautiful. John and Henry both had taken her as wife after the deaths of their angelic first wives, and no matter where she went there were reminders of Richard's two Queens. The Prince had not given up hope of winning Isabella for himself though he had not laid eyes on her since she had repulsed him and insisted on returning to France.

'Such a defiant, pretty thing,' Hal said. It was clear that his boyish imagination had been caught by her scorn, just as the public's fancy had been captured by her childish loyalty to her husband. No matter how hard the decorators worked one still came across reminders of her in the fleur-de-lys embroidered on curtains and the occasional 'Isabella' written in a book or carved on a lintel. If the campaign in France went well, Hal might still win her as his bride. The idea of welcoming the girl as her stepdaughter-in-law did not fill Joanna with any very great enthusiasm.

She would go to Langley, she decided, and wait out the winter. It would be a harsh one for there had been plague in the summer, and frost in the autumn, and more taxes had been raised to pay for the wars. Henry had hinted that she might give more to charity, but she had pretended not to understand his meaning. It was not her fault if the poor starved and suffered because of the King's dynastic ambitions. Her own fortune was steadily increasing and it made her feel warm and secure to sit calculating the interest that had accrued on her savings or fingering the long ropes of jewels with which she adorned her tall and slender figure.

Precious stones and golden coins couldn't die, or go away, or hurt one. There was no use in pretending any longer that she was a truly happy woman. Henry still came to her bedchamber and made love to her from time to time, but she sensed that his interests lay in his campaigning and, though his treatment of her was affectionate, there was in him nothing of the passion she had once dreamed her husband would display. Of her children, Marie and Jean-Pierre having made French marriages were committed to the French cause. Marie wrote brief, formal letters at New Year and Easter-tide, and Jean-Pierre never bothered to write at all. Neither did

Arthur or Jules or Richard. It was as if they blamed her for having left them behind when she had sailed to England to be married to King Henry. Yet she had done what seemed best to her at the time. The affection of the King's sons was pleasing, but she saw little of them and, since she had never been in the habit of making friends out of her waiting women, she often lacked for company.

There had been an enquiry into the deaths of the princesses, but no firm conclusions had been drawn. Joanna needed no enquiry. She was certain that the Lady Margot had poisoned them both, but there was no way of speaking her thoughts because there was no proof at all. Her gentle daughters who had ridden away on their ponies would come no more.

The winter passed slowly. There was suffering due to the poor harvest and the high prices. Snug in her apartments, Joanna gazed out at driving rain and turned back to warm her hands at the fire. It was in her opinion a pity that this foolishness of war wasn't ceased and the money spent on it put to better use.

In spring the Prince returned from Wales. Embracing him, she realised as she stepped back that he was no longer a boy. His lean frame had the hard muscle of a seasoned trooper and his black hair was cut short in a style that was doubtless practical for the wearing of a battle helmet but struck her as ugly.

'My father bids me escort you to Westminster,' he told her, accepting the cup of wine she had poured. 'We will spend Easter together.'

'How went your campaign?' She asked the question dutifully.

'We beat Glendower back and they were forced to sue for terms. I don't know if the truce will hold, but I hope so.' He grinned, suddenly looking boyish again. 'Those Celts are good fighters — not in disciplined formation but individually, dropping on our lads out of nowhere and vanishing like smoke into their mountains. Glendower had magical powers, they whisper. I am more inclined to believe that he has an excellent spy system and a sound knowledge of the terrain. I respect enemies like that more than I respect the French.'

'You have a goodly portion of French blood yourself,' she reminded him.

'But count myself English.' He gave a quick frown as if her remark jarred. 'When we regain our French possessions they will then become part of England and English laws will prevail, and I will seal the bargain by taking a French wife. You have heard that Isabella was finally coaxed to forget her loyalty to Richard and marry with her cousin of Orléans? They are saying it is a love match.'

'I am sorry for your sake,' Joanna said. 'I know how much you set your heart on winning her as your bride.'

'It would have pleased my father,' he said, 'to have wrested Richard's Queen for his son. A kind of poetic justice,

I think. Father takes his crown and I take his widow.'

'I am sorry,' she said again.

'Oh, she has a sister,' Hal said. 'Marie de Valois was given to the Church when she was a babe, but she is not yet professed. And there is always the chance that Isabella will be widowed and then I'll present my suit again. Meanwhile there are the Easter festivities ahead and we shall celebrate the spring as a family.'

He drank the rest of the wine and stood, smiling at her. He would be a strong king, she thought, and if all went well the shadow of the deposed and murdered Richard would be lifted from the Court and the whisper of 'usurper' die into silence.

10

That was the last amiable Easter, with the King coming more frequently to her bed, with herself laughing in the middle of her tall stepsons. It had even crossed her mind that she might allow herself to become pregnant. It was nearly fourteen years since her Breton physician had warned her to have no more babies, but her health was splendid now and the six years spent in England had smoothed the lines of strain from her face. It would be pleasant to have a baby, a girl perhaps whom she could spoil and keep with her for company as old age crept up and blew wrinkles into her neck. Then she reminded herself that in a few months time she would be forty and that childbearing at that age carried a greater risk than at any other time. It was better not to tempt fate by singing too loudly.

She was to look back later, trying to match effect with cause. It had begun, she thought, with an ending, with the news from France that Isabella had died in childbed after only a year's marriage.

'She was scarcely twenty-one,' Henry said. 'They say Orléans is devastated for it was a love match.'

The Court of France was in mourning as was right and proper, but what irritated Joanna was the depth of sorrow displayed in England. The exquisite child whom Richard of Bordeaux had married had proved loyal and stubborn, refusing to acknowledge the new King, insisting against all reason that Richard still lived, repudiating Prince Hal's offer of marriage with scorn. And when she had consented to marry she had made a love match with her cousin who was himself a romantic figure, handsome, brave and cultured.

In short she had acted in a way that would have had any right-minded father roaring with rage had his own daughter behaved in such a manner but, being Isabella de Valois, her behaviour was not merely forgiven but praised. It was impossible to ignore what the commons were saying. Though Joanna seldom went out in public she was only too conscious of the silence that fell when she did appear and the broadsheets being circulated found their way into the palace.

'Richard the Second has become a candidate for sainthood, it seems,' Joanna said, throwing down one such. 'He ended the Peasants' Revolt single handed at the age of fifteen! He burned Shene to the ground out of grief when Queen Anne died and it was in tribute to her memory that he next wed a child! They choose to forget that the peasants were not one whit better off after Richard spoke up for them, that he could neither hold the land his grandfather had won nor pleasure a woman.

'They remember only that he was

deposed and murdered,' Henry said.

'He could scarcely have been kept alive to act as a rallying point for the disaffected,' she argued.

'You don't understand.' Henry gave her an impatient glance. 'I would have spared him. God knows he was not fit to rule and abdicated of his own free will — almost of his own free will! He could have lived out his days in an honourable captivity, but he tried to escape. He behaved as if he were still monarch. The people loved him and they went on loving him, because he was son to the Black Prince and the Fair Maid of Kent. And he had great charm. He had only to smile and crook an elegant forefinger and men ran to do his bidding.'

Henry had no charm, Joanna thought. He had removed a weak and perverted King, had fought tenaciously to win back the lands Richard had lost, had sired a healthy family upon a first wife of impeccable lineage, had taken as second wife a royal widow with whom he lived in harmony. It made no difference. He was respected but not loved, and she herself was disliked. Daughter of Charles the Bad, the broadsheets proclaimed, with her sons by her first husband all fighting in the French cause. She had filled her household with Bretons, had conspired to have the Breton pirates released, sat in her warm palace with Anne of Bohemia's jewels about her neck while the people suffered.

'You should find the authors of these and hang them!' she said sharply, throwing down the crudely-printed sheet.

'That would not prevent people from continuing to love Richard,' Henry said. 'One would need to tear the hearts out of most of my subjects to achieve that. Even Hal remembers him with affection and regrets his death, though I swear nobody in the realm regrets it more than I do.'

He was lying to himself, of course. Had Richard lived he would never have sat safely upon the throne, but it soothed him to make believe otherwise.

'Now that Isabella is dead,' she said, 'then Hal must look elsewhere for a bride.'

'We have approached her sister, Marie,' Henry said gloomily, 'but she flung up her hands in horror and cried that she will take no earthly lord. She is set on becoming a nun as her parents intended. It is a rebuff for us from another obstinate princess. The next one, Michelle, is already betrothed to Burgundy's heir. Hal will have to take the youngest, Katharine, but first we must drive the French to the negotiating table.'

'And Hal?' Joanna questioned.

'Hal says one French girl is much the same as another.' The King frowned slightly. 'Since he returned from Wales I have seen little of him. He complains that he is short of money and cannot pay off his archers. Well, that cry goes up regularly from every commanding officer that ever lived, I suppose. Hal will have to make shift as well as he can.'

There was friction between the King and his sons where once there had been harmony. When Hal next came to Westminster Joanna seized the first opportunity to talk to him alone.

'Your father grieves that you don't visit us as often as you did,' she began mildly, taking his arm as they strolled in the long garden that ran down to the river.

'My father forgets that I have my own household and cannot always be at Court,' Hal said.

'He misses your company. He likes to talk over the campaigns with you and make plans for the next.'

'Let him pay me for the last one then,' Hal muttered, so resentfully that she was startled into exclaiming,

'My dear Hal, what ails you? Is it the death of the princess that troubles you?'

'Isabella de Valois has sisters who will serve as wives equally well.'

'If there is any way in which I can help, my dear boy,' she began, but was cut short as he shook his arm free and scowled at her.

'You can begin by not calling me boy,' he said. 'My lord father 'boys' me up hill and down dale until I am sick of it! Madam, I am not a boy. I have not been a boy since I was fifteen when my father took me to Wales to campaign! I am twenty-three years old and for nearly ten years my life has been spent between schoolroom and the saddle. The distance between the two has become greater than I can stride.'

'Naturally he wishes you to apply yourself to your studies,' she began.

'In the field,' he said impatiently, 'I apply myself to deploying my men to the best possible advantage, to foraging for rations, to doing everything in my power to gain ground without too many casualties. When I come home my father expects me to don cap and gown and study Latin! I cannot be perfect in all things. I have a life of my own to lead, and the time has come when I'll lead it as I see fit and not as I am bidden!'

'As your father's son — ' she began again.

'I am more than my father's son,' he interrupted. 'I am my own man too. He seeks to mould me into the perfect prince and display me to the people as a kind of justification for taking the throne. 'See what I have given you that Richard could not'. But he will not let me be myself!'

It was the old tale of youth rebelling against age. But Henry was not much past forty and still in his prime. Hal had tasted freedom in the valleys of Wales and would no longer submit to even a kindly yoke.

'I will speak to him,' she said. 'He was a young man himself not too long ago. I will speak on your behalf, make him understand.'

'You are a good mother to me,' Hal said. His voice had softened, but it was not hopeful.

Unhappily she timed her intervention badly. Entering the Presence Chamber she found the King walking up and down, his steps jerky, his beard bristling. He turned as she entered and said loudly,

'If you have to plead for him you may save your breath, Madam!'

'How did you — ?' Joanna stared at him.

'Because women are always foolish where boys are concerned. But this is beyond a prank! This lowers the dignity of the Crown and might even be construed as treason and he has led his brothers into it too!'

'My lord, I have no notion what you're talking about!' Joanna said in bewilderment.

'Then you must be the only person in London who is ignorant of the fact that Hal is locked up in the Fleet prison together with Thomas and John,' Henry snapped.

'Hal in prison! Surely there is some mistake!'

'None whatsoever.' The vein in the King's temple swelled and throbbed. 'Hal was arrested last night for highway robbery — he and his brothers, and half a dozen archers, all guilty of waylaying passers-by and robbing them of whatever possessions they carried. The Watch was alerted and all were carried off to gaol. They appeared before the magistrates this morning and might have been sentenced to hang had someone not recognised the princes. The chief alderman declared that, royal or not, they would all be punished and committed them to six weeks' hard labour.'

'You'll remove the man from office, of course?'

'On the contrary I sent to thank him for his honesty and courage,' Henry said. 'And I informed the magistrates that in my realm anyone who broke the law would be punished, be he prince or no!'

'Did Hal plead his rank in mitigation?'

'No, he did not.' There was a tinge

of reluctant pride in the King's voice. 'He said that he was equally guilty and would suffer with the rest! So did John and Thomas.'

'There! you see?'

'I will tell you what I see, madam!' The brief instant of relenting had vanished. 'I see that the heir to the throne is no better than a blackguard and a thief, that he is without respect for either his position or my own, that he leads his brothers into the same evil ways. It was my hope to present to this land such a prince, so godly, so upright, that men would praise the day on which I was crowned! He has thrown his gauntlet in my face and I'll not have it! I'll not have it!'

Sawing the air with his hand he tumbled a candle from its sconce and caught it as it fell, crushing the flame in his palm without appearing to notice the pain.

'My lord, surely it is to his credit that he accepts the sentence without protest?' Joanna said. 'A spell in the

Fleet will sober him, will sober them all!'

'It is to be hoped your optimism is justified,' Henry said dourly, 'but I fear that campaigning alone has gone to his head. I should not have trusted command to one so young but I sent trustworthy advisers to help him.'

'In the campaign he acquitted himself well. You said so yourself!'

'It is now that he is at home again that his true character will show itself,' Henry said. 'One day he will occupy my place. We shall see if he has in him that which is worthy to be king.'

But Hal's return to Court made matters worse, for he swaggered in wearing an insolent expression with a jest on his lips about prodigal sons that set the vein in the King's temple throbbing again.

'You have no shame for your conduct? No apology to offer?' Henry asked tightly.

'I am ashamed I could not pay my archers,' the prince said, 'and I am sorry I was caught.'

'Hal!' The King's fist crashed down upon the arm of his chair. 'You stand and defy me when you have just broken the law of the land? You face me as if it were a light matter for the heir to the throne to be locked in gaol?'

'Kings have been locked in gaol before,' Hal said.

'Meaning what?' Henry started to his feet.

'Meaning that you cannot expect me to perform penance for you.' Hal's face had whitened but not lost its insolent quality.

'Richard Plantagenet died of displeasure!'

'Aye, so it was given out,' Hal said, 'but of whose displeasure, my lord? Not his own surely? He would have been better pleased to remain alive, I think.'

'He was unfit to rule and so he died. I regret the necessity more bitterly than I can say, and have done public penance for it many times. But the

215

past is the past. Men will look to you to discern a future king who will rule wisely.'

'What concerns my archers is that they are still unpaid,' Hal put in. 'You expect me to command men but won't give me the means to pay them! You prate of justice and will not grant me one moment's freedom to be myself.'

'The young must be guided by the old!'

'Not when the old are blindfolded and heading in the wrong direction!'

'You will apologise for that!'

They were both on their feet shouting, lips drawn back from their teeth, their eyes hard. Between them Joanna hovered anxiously, her head moving from one to the other.

'Oh, hell and damnation!' The prince threw his arms up in a gesture of complete frustration.

'And you are bound for both!' his father shouted.

'Then, with your royal permission,

I'll ride to my manor of Cheylesmoor and gather some good company for the journey,' Hal snapped and, turning on his heel, strode out.

'Hal! Hal, wait!' Joanna picked up her skirts and flew after him, scattering a group of open mouthed pages.

'Wait for what? To be put down and treated like dirt because I will not crawl to my father and lick his boots?' The prince tugged free of her detaining grasp.

'Your father loves you and wants to have you stand high in men's opinion!'

'Then let him give me money so that I can pay off my archers, and let him grant me a little space in which I can be myself,' Hal said stonily.

'The French campaigns have depleted the Privy Purse. Many of his own troops remain unpaid.'

'Cannot you help me out?' he asked bluntly.

'Hal, dear, I wish I could!' The familiar panic had clutched at her stomach and she took a step back, twisting her fingers. 'But my own revenues are greatly reduced this year. I shall have trouble in paying my own servants, I swear!'

'It makes no matter.' He patted her shoulder and turned away whistling for his horse.

After that on the rare occasions when he came to Court he stayed for the shortest possible time, addressed his father with cold civility, and walked out without permission if any comment was passed on his mode of life. What that life was had become common gossip that elbowed even Joanna's fancied iniquities off the broadsheets. At Cheylesmoor Manor in Cheshire he held miniature Court, drinking and roistering and keeping the neighbours awake with the noise that continued until dawn. His brothers, save Humphrey the youngest, roistered with him, often galloping their horses through the town at top speed while they aimed their arrows at windows, inn signs and weathercocks, screaming like Celtic savages when their arrows found a mark.

'His boon companion is Oldcastle,' Henry said, drawing down the corners of his mouth in displeasure. 'A reprobate knight if ever there was one — Oh! I'd not deny his courage on the field, but his drinking and wenching off it is a scandal! And there are worse than Oldcastle with whom he spends his time. Common mercenaries and loose women who encourage him to wilder excesses. His name has become a byword for intemperance, for lechery, for vandalism!'

In his agitation he had picked up a paper-knife and was stabbing his own hand over and over, the sharp points raising drops of blood.

'My lord! you are hurting yourself!' Joanna exclaimed.

'What? Oh, 'tis nothing!' He threw down the knife with a little clatter. 'But these sheets of — one cannot call them scandal for what they say is true — they prick my heart. Hal drags our good name in the dust like a forgotten saddle! All my life I have lived decently, first with my beloved Mary and then with you. God knows I have done penance for Richard's murder over and over, have pitted myself against the Welsh and the French in an effort to win back the lands he lost — and my son turns upon me. He falls down drunk in the streets, takes bad women into his bed, consorts with low-living archers.'

'And the people love him for it,' Joanna thought suddenly. 'That is what gnaws at you! The people do not love kings who bring them good law and set an example of domestic morality. They love the weak Richards and the wild Hals because in their frailties they see their own diminished.'

There was nothing of this that she could say to the King who had picked up the knife again and was pricking his hand with the sharp point. He had put weight on since he had ceased campaigning, and his complexion was pasty. His beard had recently been trimmed into the new short point and when he pushed back his fur-lined cap she could see the hair receding at his temples, and the veins bulging blackly.

'My lord, are you feeling well?' she asked sharply.

'I have been somewhat distempered of late,' he admitted.

'Then you must see a physician,' she said.

'If you wish.' He spoke dully, his temper falling into ashes, his eyes lowered to his bleeding hand.

A few weeks later the King sent for her when she was seated at her accounts. It was unusual for him to request her presence so formally, and she hurried to the Presence Chamber at once, fearing some new escapade of the Prince's had come to his ears.

He had dismissed his attendants and sat alone by the fire, his chin on his hand. As she entered and sank into a curtsy he turned his head towards her and she was shocked by the look on his face.

'My dear, what is it? What has happened?' she demanded.

'I have consulted my physicians,' he said bleakly.

'They have told you something disturbing?' She went towards him but he put up a hand to ward her off.

'You are on your honour not to repeat this,' he said. 'On your honour, Joanna, as my Queen.'

'Of course,' she said, bewildered.

'Swear it, Joanna,' he said.

'I swear it.' She clasped her hands tightly together, controlling her trembling.

'The physicians tell me that I am sick, that before long it will be necessary for me to withdraw from public life,' he said.

'You are seriously ill?' She looked at him in alarm. 'There are other physicians, sir. It is always wise to seek a second opinion.'

'On this matter there can be no other opinion.' His voice was calm, but his mouth twisted as if he were gripped by some unbearable anguish. 'You have been a good wife to me, Joanna. I have enjoyed your company. Now you will go to Langley and wait there. I will not have you burdened by the care of a dying man.'

'Dying! Surely you exaggerate!' She strove to keep her voice cool and light. 'At forty-five a man does not give in to the idea of dying as if there were no remedies! If you are sick, then my place is with you!'

'You will go to Langley or to Havering-atte-Bower if that pleases you more,' he said. 'I will have you obey me in this.'

'But you have not told me,' she began, and stopped, her stomach heaving as he leaned and held his hand so close to the fire that by rights he should not have been able to bear the pain. Now, backing from him slowly, she saw with the horror of full knowledge the significance of the whitening skin, the slight bloating of the face, the hand that felt no pain.

'You will not weep and make a fuss,' he said sternly. 'We have lived in dignity and harmony, and we will end thus.'

Very slowly, her head high, she swept him a deep curtsy and thought, 'If I loved him this moment would break my heart.'

11

All her life she had stood at windows waiting for news. On this occasion she was at Westminster and no matter what tidings reached her they would bring pain.

'You are my dearest stepmother,' the new King had said when she went to kiss his hands. 'As my late father honoured you, so will I honour you. When I am absent from the realm you will be Regent.'

'Do you plan to be absent, Sire?' She gave him a troubled glance.

'I plan to gain back all the territories Richard lost in France,' he said.

'But Hal — ' She bit back the old nickname, seeing that it embarrassed him. 'Henry, have you not considered that treaties are better than campaigns?'

'Charles the Sixth is not in his right mind three-quarters of the time,' he interrupted. 'His Queen is a noted adulteress, flaunting her affairs. Nobody can be certain all her children are his. The Dauphin is a weak fool who spends his days in wenching and gambling and his nights cowering from thunderstorms. France deserves better than that — and most of France is mine by hereditary right anyway!'

It was the old argument for waging a war that would waste revenue and cost lives. Joanna stifled a sigh.

'I was bred to be both soldier and scholar,' Henry was continuing. 'When the battle trumpets sound it is time for me to put away my books and lead my men to victory.'

But he was sounding the trumpets himself, she thought irritably. The wild young Hal had hardened into a man who dreamed of conquest.

And the entire country was behind him. War-fever had gripped even the urchins in the street who took turns at being French or English and banged at one another with staves. The English side, Joanna noted wryly, always won.

'I would have you write to your sons, bidding them aid me as their father aided my father,' Henry said.

'Sire! they are grown men now and not mine to command,' she said in dismay.

'There is amity between England and Brittany,' he reminded her. 'The Duke — '

'Jean-Pierre is wed to Joan of France. You cannot expect him to take up arms against his father-in-law!'

'Why not?' There was a rare glint of humour in her stepson's face. 'I am taking up arms against him and I hope to make him my father-in-law too.'

'You will seek the hand of the Princess Katharine?'

The child, Isabella, who had remained loyal to the murdered Richard, had died herself and there was no further need to envy her, but her youngest sister was still unmarried. Joanna looked at the King with some curiosity. It seemed from the way in which he had spoken that he had transferred his affections for political reasons, taking shadow for substance. She could not help feeling a trifle sorry for Katharine. Yet hers was the common lot of high-born girls. It had been Joanna's lot too, save that John of Brittany had proved an uncommonly kindly husband.

'Will the French King agree to give you his daughter?' she asked.

'By the time I have finished waging war in his country,' Henry said grimly, 'he will be begging me to take her. Madam, use your good offices for me with your sons.'

Only three sons now, she thought sadly. The sickly Jules had died only a few months before the late King. She had not seen the others for years, and Marie had allied herself completely with her husband and the French.

Her letters had been quite fruitless. Jean-Pierre had informed her that rather than take arms against father-in-law or stepbrother he chose to remain neutral. Arthur, in defiance of the fealty he had sworn to the English King, had ridden to Paris and thrown in his lot with the Valois, and Richard had not troubled to reply at all.

'It is not your fault, Madam mother,' Henry said, but there was disappointment in his tone. It was plain he had expected more from her intervention.

He had, however, left her and his brother Bedford as co-regents, though there was little enough to do after the fleet set sail save wait for news of victory or defeat.

'And how shall I hope?' she thought. 'When my children sit in the enemy camp?'

The prospect of hand-to-hand combat between her son and stepson crossed her mind and was so appalling that she shut it out.

'Herald Antelope is riding in at the gallop, Your Grace!' one of her pages hurried in to say. 'It is victory, I think.'

'But for whom?' Joanna thought as

she turned swiftly and made her way to the Presence Chamber where groups of servants were hastily gathering.

''Tis a splendid victory, Your Grace!'

Antelope, still cloaked and spurred, fell to his knee before her. 'Three days since, on St Crispin's Day, our forces engaged with the French and were triumphant. Many thousands are dead on the enemy side and others taken prisoner. His Grace is safe and unharmed.'

'Thanks be to God,' she said mechanically.

'His Grace bade me ride like the wind the moment ship touched shore,' the herald said. 'I near killed my mount in getting here. There will be many rich ransoms from the battle and maybe a truce since the best of the French knights are slain.'

'Who?' Her voice was sharp.

'D'Alençon was killed in the first mêlée, Your Grace, and went down under a rain of battle-axes.' His enthusiastic voice faltered as he recalled suddenly that D'Alençon had been the Queen's son-in-law.

Marie's husband killed. Joanna swallowed over a lump in her throat, remembering how Marie had begged to be sent to France so that she could be reared in luxury. It had been a happy marriage and a fruitful one, and now Marie was a widow.

'Madam, your son, the Lord Arthur, is taken prisoner,' Antelope said.

Joanna closed her eyes briefly. 'Prisoner' meant alive, but Arthur had broken his oath of fealty which was a serious matter.

'We must make preparations to welcome them home,' she said, schooling her voice to calmness. 'You have informed the Council?'

'I rode directly to you, Madam, His Grace bade me,' he told her.

Her stepson did not then hold her responsible for her son's dereliction. She felt the colour beginning to come back into her cheeks.

'Go to the Council at once. Milord

Bedford will be chafing for some word. This is wonderful news you bring. The whole country will rejoice.'

And she must rejoice with them. Her daughter was widowed, her son a disgraced prisoner, but the Queen Dowager of England must not allow divided loyalties to temper her delight. Nobody must be able to say that Joanna was less than whole-hearted in her support of her stepson.

A month later, with bells ringing out from every steeple and banners fluttering from every ledge and chimney, the victors processed through London to the Palace of Westminster. Though it was November and cold the air was dry and crisp, and a pale sun tipped with gold the spears of the marching men.

Joanna, looking down from a balcony upon the gleaming spears and shields, the fluttering pennants, the heralds in their scarlet and gold, could not prevent a wave of excitement from rippling through her. There was, after all, a certain charm about victory. Since early morning people had been thronging into the streets to drink wine and munch roasted apples and chestnuts, and tell one another that Harry the Fifth would gain back all that the second Richard had lost.

The cheers were deafening now, which meant that the King was approaching. He rode into view flanked by his brothers, gleaming circlet atop his helmet, a scarlet cloak swinging from armour that was dented in several places. He was the warrior King, with nothing of the scholar about him now.

Behind him the knights and barons jostled on their horses, stirrup against stirrup, their squires riding behind them. And behind them, rank upon rank, came the archers, carrying the new-fashioned longbows, the quivers on their backs bristling like porcupines. Some of them were limping or bandaged; many had doxies clinging to their arms.

Below Joanna a girl stepped out, speaking urgent words to one of the men. He shook his head and pointed a thumb towards the ground, and the girl turned away, her hands covering her face, her drooping shoulders telling of a sweetheart who had not returned from France. She was fortunate to be allowed to show her feelings, the Queen thought, and moved her head a little, leaning into the shadow of the canopy as the prisoners came by.

There were many prisoners, though she had heard a rumour that some of them had had their throats cut on the field since they were not likely to bring much ransom. The crowd cheered them almost as loudly as they had cheered the King, a circumstance which struck her as ironic. She tried to pick out Arthur, but there were too many heads bobbing below. In any case she had not seen him for ten years. It was doubtful if she would recognise him.

'Your Grace?'

One of her ladies was speaking to her. It was time to greet the King formally, to offer her congratulations on his victory.

She had dressed with care in a new gown of dark blue velvet with sleeves of white fur. Under the horned headdress of white and gold her face was carefully painted. She moved with conscious dignity through the corridors to the Great Hall where the King stood upon the dais, flanked by his brothers.

'Your Grace, this is a very happy day,' Joanna began, but Henry had stepped down, taking both her hands as he embraced her.

'A happy homecoming, Madam Mother. I am told you and my good brother Bedford kept the realm at peace during my absence.'

'Your Grace had other business,' she said, smiling.

'Equally important for the realm. It was a splendid battle!' His eyes glowed and there was enthusiasm in his voice. 'We fought near a small chateau called

Agincourt and so I decreed the battle to be named. It has a ring to it.'

'Of English steel,' said Bedford, and Henry turned to clap his brother upon the shoulder.

'Say rather English yew, for it was the longbows saved the day,' he said. 'The flower of French chivalry fell at Agincourt. They fought well. Oh, they outnumbered us but they lacked leadership. I myself walked among the common soldiers the night before, talked with them, told them what strategy I had planned. They appreciated that. A man will fight more valiantly for a leader who has acknowledged his existence.'

Did all men fight their battles over and over again? Joanna, moving to her place at the high table where a banquet was spread, wondered if she was going to become as sick of the word 'Agincourt' as she had been of 'Aurey', when John had relived his hours of glory over and over again.

It being Advent the meal was of fish

with oysters, crabs and lobsters followed by perch and salmon garnished with truffles and watercress and sugar cakes with the banners of England iced on their surfaces. Henry had removed his armour and was now in a tunic of dark green embroidered with golden lilies. Above the jewelled collar his face was smiling and cheerful. Perhaps now was the right time to broach the subject that tore at her mind.

Leaning towards him she said, under cover of the general conversation,

'Sire, concerning my son, Lord Arthur — ?'

'He is prisoner.' Henry spoke curtly, the smile fading from his face as if a hand had wiped it away.

'I know. I wondered if ransom had been set.'

'I do not ransom traitors.' His voice was crisp, like bread breaking. 'My stepbrother swore fealty to me and then fought for France. That is treason and liable to the extreme penalty of the law.'

For a moment the banqueting hall swung crazily round. She gave a small moan deep in her throat, her hand shaking so violently that the goblet she held spattered red drops over the white tablecloth.

'He is not yet two and twenty,' she whispered.

'Old enough to know the meaning of loyalty.' His face softened slightly as he saw her distress. 'However we do not intend to proceed to extremes. He will be lodged in the Tower until my pleasure is made known.'

'Am I to be granted interview?' She kept her voice steady with an effort.

'Later, in your apartments.' He nodded in a more cordial fashion, then resumed his account of the battle.

Nibbling at a piece of marchpane Joanna longed for the interminable evening to be over. This was a male Court with no room in it for tender glances or sweet music, and she had had little of either during her life.

'D'Alençon's charge was a noble

one,' Henry was saying. 'Had it not been for young Tydyr here he'd have cloven my helmet in two.'

He jerked his head towards a young man who sat at the end of the table.

The young man, who was shabbily clad, had chestnut hair falling almost to his shoulders and looked more minstrel than soldier.

'The Welsh fought well,' Gloucester said.

'In this campaign I was glad they were on my side,' Henry said. 'They fought like demons for Glendower ten years back, though Owen there would have been too young. But I'd liefer make a brave enemy my body squire than a false friend.'

He hits at my son again, Joanna thought, but Arthur was reared in France from the time he was ten and paid fealty only by proxy to the English monarch. Henry does not consider that. He sees only England and a dream of French conquest.

'Owen there can sing like an angel

as well as fight like a devil,' Henry said. 'He's of the line of Davy Gam, he tells me. Mayhap I'll send him to do my wooing when I court the fair Katharine.'

There was a burst of hearty masculine laughter. Joanna, smiling faintly, thought, 'Henry does not know it but he has more in common with Richard the Second than is good for a man who thinks of taking a wife.'

The King was rising, the doors being opened to admit the crowd of spectators in the yard who would finish off the victuals left by their betters and dare one another to sit in the royal chair. Joanna rose too, summoning her attendants with a crooked forefinger. It was not to her taste to sit and be gaped at by the mob. It was a sad thing but she had never been popular with the English. Once or twice, being carried through the streets in her litter, she had seen one of the bystanders make the sign against the evil eye, and known that her father's evil reputation extended even here long after his death. By now those same people would know her son had broken oath and fought on the other side.

She left through a side door which led to a maze of apartments, staircases and courtyards. The palace of Westminster sprawled along the river and was more like a small town than a royal dwelling with its cottages, its chapels, its booths where enterprising citizens sold goods to the hundreds of servants and clerics who thronged its draughty chambers. She had considered Brittany an uncomfortable place until she had come to Westminster

In her own apartments the fires were lit and the shutters closed against the November night, but the sound of revelry still drifted up from the river. People would be dancing and singing until dawn, full of pride in the exploits of their warrior King. It wouldn't enter their foolish heads that taxes would be increased to pay for it. One person would not be rejoicing. She remembered the girl she had noticed who had questioned the archer and turned away, weeping. Joanna would have liked to talk to her, to tell her that love was an illusion and never outlasted middle age, but the girl would not have believed her anyway.

'Your Grace, the Lord Arthur is being escorted here.'

One of her pages came into the room, having paused to receive a message from a hurrying chaplain.

'Already? But I am not prepared. After ten years — ' Suddenly she was in a fluster, shivering with a mixture of excitement and apprehension. In ten years she had changed, her delicate prettiness settling into plumpness, her gait becoming more stately than graceful.

The approach of marching feet broke into her flurry of protestations. She drew back, her hand seeking the arm of her chair, bracing herself for this reunion with the little boy who had ridden on his pony into France.

The young man entering looked as

John of Brittany must have looked when young, tall, slim, darkly handsome. She took a step forward, but he had already embraced one of her ladies, exclaiming,

'My lady mother, you look not a day older!'

'Oh, Arthur, don't you recognise your own mother?'

Exasperated tears sparkled in her eyes as he hastily released the lady and stared at her.

'My lady mother?' He looked at her uncertainly.

'Such a son, not to know me!' she cried, half laughing, half crying.

'It has been such a long time.' He went to her then, embracing her awkwardly as if they were strangers.

'You have grown,' she said foolishly, and with the saying of it he was her son again with the strangeness gone and the ten years shrunk to nothing between them.

'And you are so grandly attired 'tis no wonder than I didn't know you!'

She had forgotten the shabby clothes she had worn as Duchess of Brittany, the paucity of her jewels. Yet in those days she had not needed them.

'The King granted this meeting.' She waved her attendants away, drawing him nearer to the fire. 'You are to be sent to the Tower.'

'Aye, so I was told. Well, it's better than the block with which he originally threatened me,' he said wryly.

'How can you joke? And what possessed you to fight for France when your allegiance is to England?'

'Because your late husband conferred on me the earldom of Richmond? This is the first time I ever set foot in England!'

'An oath is an oath.'

'Made by proxy when I was a boy? Mother, I spent my childhood in Brittany and my boyhood in Paris. What reason do I have for supporting England?'

'You should have stayed neutral like Jean-Pierre.'

'Jean-Pierre has no stomach for fighting save with his wife,' Arthur said with a grin. 'He resents it that you tied Brittany into an English alliance when he was still too young to govern his Duchy.'

'I acted as I thought right at the time,' she said defensively. 'Henry of England offered security.'

'He offered a chain by which he hoped to tie Brittany to his ambitions in France,' he said impatiently. 'Had we come with you to England it might have worked out differently, but you sent us into France. Are we to be blamed because our loyalties are divided?'

'Yours do not appear to be since you fought for France!' She broke off, tears starting into her eyes again. 'After ten years we spend our time in arguing politics! Arthur, tell me of other things. Have you seen Marie recently?'

'She was happy with D'Alençon.' His young face was sombre. 'God knows how she has taken the news of his death. It needed six men to kill him.'

Always battles and news of dying. Joanna said quickly,

'Tell me of King Charles. When I was a girl in France he was always very kind to me.'

'The King has fits of mania that grow longer, but he is always gentle. It is a tragedy that his mind is ill balanced.' Arthur hesitated. 'There is a streak of madness in the Valois blood — and his Queen is no help. Isabeau de Bavaire would drive a saint to frenzy.'

'Henry seeks the Princess Katharine.'

'So that he can work upon King Charles to disinherit his own sons and bequeath the crown to any child of such a marriage, in defiance of Salic law. My royal stepbrother has dynastic ambitions.'

'Pray keep such thoughts to yourself,' Joanna begged nervously. 'If Henry chose to be vindictive you might yet end on the scaffold.'

'I will be as diplomatic as an archbishop,' he promised, 'and sit in a dungeon instead.'

'Oh, surely not!' She gave him a horrified glance. 'You will be lodged more comfortably than that!'

'Provided I can pay.' He made a face that reminded her of the times when, as a little boy, he had been forced to take medicine. 'I cannot expect to be ransomed, and the King has made it clear I am not up for ransom anyway, and I scarcely think that he will be anxious to grant me any luxuries.'

'I can give you a thousand nobles. My rents are in from Brittany!'

'That is good of you, mother.' His tone was one of such transparent surprise that she said indignantly,

'Did you think I would allow my own son to languish in some hole below the water line?'

'I have heard it whispered that you are apt to be somewhat near.'

'If you had been forced to live on the meagre allowance your father doled out to me you would understand why I don't squander money now,' she said. 'As it is I am often forced to wait

247

because Jean-Pierre is late in sending me my rents.'

'I can see that you are in a sad way, Mother,' he commented, glancing at her furred sleeves, the diamonds that edged the gold lace stretched over the horns of her headdress.

It was all going wrong, she thought miserably. The reunion had been spent in arguing about politics and money. Clearly her sons blamed her for having left them behind when she had married the English King. Their chief loyalties now lay with France. The little boys who had practised with wooden swords in the courtyard had ridden away on the ponies and would never come again. Arthur had not even recognised her.

It was almost a relief when the escort returned and he rose to embrace her.

'You will not forget the thousand nobles?' were his parting words and somehow they summed up the whole interview.

'I will see that it is sent to you at

once for your greater comfort in the Tower,' she said, and felt no longer the inclination to weep.

In a way Henry was closer to her now than her own children. She was surprised and touched when he came to her a few days later with a great bolt of sapphire velvet carried by two pages who panted behind him for the King walked briskly everywhere and was always impatient with stragglers.

'A gift from France, Madam Mother.' He bent to peck at her cheek. 'The ladies too deserve a share of the spoils of war.'

'You are generous, Sire.' She ran her hand over the thick pile of the velvet with keen appreciation.

'I would have you wear it when you greet my bride.'

'Is it to be an alliance then?' She shot him an anxious glance. 'Will King Charles give you his daughter?'

'I intend to take her.' Henry's voice was flat and businesslike. 'Charles will have to talk peace with me sooner or later. His finest leaders fell or were captured at Agincourt. His kingdom is shrinking and he will be forced to offer terms, provided he is in a state to understand what I am talking about. He is not in his right mind half the time but fortunately his Queen is.'

'And the princess?'

'She is spoken of as healthy and fairly intelligent. If she resembles her sister, the late Isabella, then she is also beautiful.'

'I wondered if she had expressed any opinion,' Joanna ventured.

'Opinion?' Henry echoed blankly. 'Why, what opinion could she have? She will marry where she is bidden, but her mind will be more inclined to it after she hears rumours that I am considering marrying one of the Aragon princesses.'

'Are you?' Joanna asked.

He shook his head.

'I will have Katharine in the end. She will bear me a son who will unite the thrones of England and France. I am past thirty and must consider the future.'

There was a coldness in him that chilled her. She remembered the wild youth flung into gaol for his exploits and how earnestly she had striven to keep the peace between him and his exasperated father. Had the coldness been there all the time and she had not seen it? Despite the wildness of his youth she had never heard of any scandal involving women. Glancing at the thin lips in the handsome austere face she could not help feeling a pang of pity for the young Katharine, destined to be handed over as part of the spoils of war for the express purpose of begetting an heir.

12

Fifty was a good age for other people, Joanna reflected wryly, gazing critically into the mirror, but it was not a good age for oneself to be. Her golden hair was now plentifully streaked with white and there were lines beginning to show all too plainly in her neck. She had also put on a little weight though her ladies assured her that this was becoming. Certainly her skin was still clear if one overlooked the faint crepeness of her eyelids. But there was no sense in pretending she was a young woman any longer.

Six years since Henry had died, his ravaged features concealed by a thick veil. He had been proud of his good looks too. It was the worst irony that leprosy should have eaten his flesh, turning health into white corruption. Theirs had been a good marriage of friendship and shared interests, and she had had the wisdom to realise that she could never replace his first wife in his affections, though there had been times when she had grown a little weary of hearing about Mary de Bohun's perfections.

Henry's death had been a grief but not a tragedy. His bequests to her had been generous. She now owned the castles of Leeds, Langley and Havering Bower, and the revenues of several manors. The days of scrimping and saving in the little stronghold of Vannes were far behind her but she found it impossible to forget them. There were nights even now when she would lie wakeful going over the accounts in her mind.

Thinking of that brought back a disquieting conversation she had recently had with the King. He had visited her at Havering Bower which, with its wooded prospects and peach orchards, was one of her favourite residences. He had looked tired and drawn, older than his thirty-two years, with little trace about him of the heedless youngling whom she had met when she had first come into England. Now he looked like a seasoned warrior who grows tired of the struggle.

She had broached the subject and received an impatient frown.

'Not weary of the struggle, Your Grace, for I was bred to battle, but sick to death of the wrangling that goes on between encounters! The King of France is in his right mind and wishes to talk peace! The King of France is out of his wits and Burgundy will not yield! I feel as if I were on a seesaw that goes up and down, up and down — and I am no nearer my marriage with Katharine. She will be eighteen soon, ripe for the corruptions of her mother's household, unless I can get her away.'

'You are marrying her to save her soul? My dear Harry!' Joanna raised her plucked eyebrows and smiled, but her stepson's face was void of humour.

'Since I was a boy,' he said, 'I have been trying and failing to get a wife! First your own daughter who was given instead to Alençon, and then Isabella who would not have me, and Marie who declared herself wedded to her vocation — I must get me an heir or everything I worked for will crash down when I am gone.'

'You have some affection for Lady Katharine?' Joanna asked, a trifle sharply.

'I saw her only on the one occasion and spoke with her but briefly,' he answered. 'She is very beautiful — no, I use the wrong word for she is small and thin with sallow skin and a long nose, but she has eyes with golden flecks in them and there are strands of gold in her hair so that when she turns her head one sees them glint. She is — fascinating. When I saw her I knew that I would not be content until she was my wife.'

'And she was willing?'

Henry looked faintly puzzled.

'She will wed where she is bidden,' he said at last, 'but she likes me. I felt it in her. What is needed now is a full-scale thrust into the heart of France, but I lack the wherewithal. I can raise no more taxes for a year or two and Parliament is reluctant to grant me another loan.' He paused, sliding a glance at her.

'My own revenues fluctuate,' she said uneasily.

'You have holdings in Brittany inherited from your first husband.'

'They are not destined for the purchase of arms and the hiring of mercenaries,' she countered. 'Anyway Jean-Pierre deals with my affairs.'

'He is married to the Lady Katharine's sister.'

'Which puts him in a difficult position. He has always maintained a strict neutrality.'

'Which is not to his credit,' Henry said. 'I am disappointed in your sons, Madam. The one has never lifted a finger to help us, and the other broke his oath of fealty and fought at Agincourt with the Dauphin's men.'

'He was sore wounded and taken prisoner,' Joanna said.

Tears had rushed into her eyes. The sad truth was that those of her children who had not died were proving a disappointment. Jean-Pierre idled away his time in Brittany with his French wife, Arthur was still in captivity for his part at Agincourt, and Richard had gone to Navarre where he spent his time in wenching. Marie she had not seen since she had gone to France to be reared in the Alençon household. It was a shock to recall that the eager, pretty child was now thirty and a widow, her husband having died at Agincourt.

'Count Arthur is well treated, out of respect for you,' Henry said now.

'I am grateful for it.' She looked across the table to where he sat, trying to find some trace of the heedless youth in the hard-faced man. 'I will be honest with you. My sons were so young when I sent them into the custody of my uncle of Burgundy that I have always felt closer to you and your brothers.'

'Then you will lend me the revenues I need to launch a full-scale invasion?' he said.

Suddenly she was no longer in the warm, luxuriously appointed supper-room of Havering Bower but in the draughty castle of Vannes, with her husband, John.

'My dear, the rents this season must be directed to the defence of my realm, not wasted on jewellery and dresses. Perhaps next year — '

Always next year, while she wore the same gowns season after season and fretted about her daughters' dowers.

'Madam?'

She returned from the past to find Henry staring at her.

'I'm sorry.' She rose abruptly, her voice harsh as she held back panic. 'I have no money to spare on invasions. None at all! I wish you success in your winning of your bride, but I can lend nothing.'

He had taken his leave soon afterwards, but it had been a cool farewell. At the time she had been relieved to have no argument, but now and then she felt a twinge of uneasiness. She shrugged it away, took another less than satisfied glance in the mirror, and rose. Fifty or not, she was at least fashionably attired. The houppelande of dove-grey silk flecked with silver crescents was bordered in ermine, the wide-horned headdress covered in pale green that matched the hanging sleeves with their dagged edges of silver. The new styles were so extravagant that there were sermons preached against them in church. The young men were no less fantastic, their point-toed shoes curling upwards, their short capes patterned with stars.

It was the end of July and bees hung heavy on the air. The peaches were ripening and the roses were wide-petalled, like women at the peak of their loveliness before autumn set in. Joanna made the comparison in her own mind and disliked it. One of her ladies was by the sundial, talking with a young squire. The two stood, fingertips touching, the girl's head inclined to hear the young man's whisper. It was the French garden of long ago when Oliver de Clisson had kissed her. Now there would be no more embraces. Tears pricked her eyes again and she thought impatiently,

'As my courses grow scanty my tears flow more readily.'

To have been the girl in the garden, to have become the woman staring through the window — there was sadness in that and a dull, brooding resentment. She turned away sharply, fumbling for the key at her waist. One of the inner chambers at Havering Bower was entered only by herself and her two pages, lads in their early teens whom she had taken under her wing. Roger Colles was the son of a serf and would never earn the forty pounds a year necessary before one could be invested with knighthood.

Petronel Brocart had a face as delicate as a girl's and a club-foot. Both were intelligent and discreet, with a feeling for that which lay beyond reason. To none of her sons had she confided any of the lessons imparted to her by her father before she had gone to France as a hostage for his good behaviour. Many of them she had forgotten herself, or not wanted to remember, but the books he had left her were still there, most of them annotated in his own hand. She had opened them half fearfully at first, and then the ancient words with their insistent, brain-numbing rhythms, the charts showing the phases of the moon and rising of the planets, the circles and pentagrams, became, by degrees, as familiar as they once had been.

'Bark of the willow is good for aches in the joints.' She had schooled Roger and Petronel carefully behind the locked door of the room where she kept the dark crystal under the black velvet, the jars of pounded herbs, the ring-stone. 'And for the toothache you must take clove. It burns out the pain. For disorder of the heart the foxglove is most useful, but only a very little. It is a dangerous flower that can kill as well as cure.'

Her father had used such herbs for killing. She wondered sometimes, as she turned the pages, if she could ever hate anyone sufficiently to kill them. Yet killing came often for other reasons than hate.

'I was fond of Richard,' Henry had told her. 'Had he been a good king I'd have served him as faithfully as my father did. But he was weak and foolish, with no manhood in him. It was expedient for him to die.'

That had been a chilling phrase. She had thought about it often, thought of Richard so beloved by his child-bride, Isabella, whose prayerbook she had found on the day of her own coronation. She had been aware that, as Henry had grown older, the murder of his cousin had troubled his conscience. Yet she guessed that, had the opportunity arisen to live his life again, he would have done exactly the same things.

'We are locked into our own natures,' she thought, 'and there is little we can do to alter them.' So Richard would have died over and over 'for expediency', her father brewed poisons instead of healing lotions, and she herself had known only one kiss in a garden.

The room was cool and dim, sleepy with spices. She went over to the table on which one of the books lay open, next to a small bowl in which she had been mixing a camomile with a few grains of white lead. The resulting paste was reputed to soften and whiten the complexion. She looked down into the bowl doubtfully. The quantity of lead advised seemed meagre, but if she experimented with more the result might be disastrous. If her father had been here he would not have hesitated to use the concoction on a serving wench, but she could never bring herself to experiment on living creatures.

She turned away, restless, though usually simply being in this private chamber gave her a sense of purpose. The long day lagged ahead. In a week's time it would be full moon and at that period she always felt uneasy as if she had a skin too few. On full-moon nights it was hard to sleep and she often rose, pacing until dawn. She reached for the handbell and rang it with a touch of impatience. Both Roger and Petronel were supposed to remain within earshot. By now, even without summons, one of them should have put in an appearance.

Neither Roger's quick, decided step nor the uneven gait of Petronel responded to the jangling. Frowning, Joanna stepped to the door, unlocked it and locked it again as she passed through. Going down the winding stone steps she was conscious of an uneasy churning in the pit of her stomach though full moon was still a week away.

One of her ladies was at work on a small tapestry in the solar. She began to rise but Joanna waved her back.

'Margaret, have you seen Roger or Petronel?' she enquired.

'Not since this morning, Your Grace. They were going towards the chapel. I believe that Father Randolf wished to see them. Shall I go and look?' Margaret's eager tone hinted at boredom with her needlework.

'I'll walk that way myself.' Joanna nodded smilingly and went out again.

At Havering Bower the chapel was some distance from the main building, a circumstance that occasioned some grumbling among the household in rainy weather, but provided a pleasant walk in summer for the way led through the rose gardens. Adjacent to the chapel was the small house where Father Randolf lived in what he termed 'a sylvan retreat, Your Grace, that suits me better than I can say. I have had my fill of palaces and pomp, and long only for simplicity.'

265

Simplicity, Joanna reflected with an inward chuckle, meant, in Father Randolf's case, a study with an Ottoman rug on the floor, a prayer-desk inlaid with ivory, and first choice of the harvest fruits. It was a small price to pay for a confessor who gave the lightest of penances, never investigated her reading matter, and tactfully assumed illness when she occasionally missed a mass. He was, in her opinion, a civilised man, but she wondered why he wanted to see Roger and Petronel. The pair of them had, it was true, a cheerfully irreverent attitude to religion, but it was kept within bounds.

The chapel, when she glanced within, was deserted, the house silent and shuttered. That, in itself, was odd. At this hour Father Randolf was usually to be found pottering in his garden or, having abandoned rake and hoe, reclining with his feet up and a straw hat shielding his face from the sun.

She called to Hannah, the maidservant

who did the rough work for the priest and whom she now saw approaching around the corner of the barn.

'Where is Father?'

The girl, dropping a hurried curtsy, came forward, twisting her apron between her finger.

'If it please Your Grace — ' She had a thick country accent, difficult to follow, though Joanna's English was fluent. 'It it please you, Father's not here.'

'I can see that for myself!' Joanna said sharply. 'Where has he gone?'

'He went off with some men.' The girl tortured the apron more violently.

'What men? Where did they go?'

'Don't know, Your Grace. They rode off.' The girl hesitated, clearly shy at being addressed by the Queen, and added, 'Master Colles and Master Brocart went too.'

There was no making any sense of it. Dismissing Hannah, she frowned at the shuttered house, took another glance in the deserted chapel and retraced her steps slowly through the gardens. There was, of course, no reason why Father Randolf should not have gone riding though she couldn't fathom who his escort might be, but her pages had no business to leave the premises without leave. She had never been a harsh mistress but she was an exacting one, never content to wink her eye at any dereliction of duty. Moreover both Roger and Petronel were dutiful lads, proud of their close attendance upon her. She guessed that it compensated the one for his lowly birth and the other for his crippled foot.

There were men riding into the courtyard, sunlight glinting on their armour. She glanced at them idly, then continued on her way along the flagged path to where the roses spread themselves in a final blaze of glory against the wall. Visitors were uncommon in her household for since Henry's death she had withdrawn into private life.

'Your Grace? Oh, Your Grace!'

Margaret, her needle-work abandoned, came running out, hair escaping from its caul.

'My dear Meg, what in the world ails you?' Joanna demanded.

'Milord of Bedford is here, with a warrant for your arrest!' the other gasped out.

'Don't be foolish,' Joanna said blankly.

'Madam, he's here. He told me you are under arrest and none of us must leave the premises,' Margaret insisted.

'You misheard. Where is the Duke?'

'In the solar, Your Grace, and his men are all over the house!'

Joanna quickened her step, entering through the side door that opened into the corridor at the end of which the solar provided more privacy and warmth than either hall or Presence Chamber.

'My dear John, what on earth is all this — ?' Her voice trailed away as her eye fell on the two guards who closed in behind her as she entered the room.

'Your Grace, I have a warrant for your arrest.' He had risen from the desk at which he was seated, favouring her with a curt bow.

'Is this a joke? It's not April,' she began.

'No joke,' he said flatly.

'I don't understand.' Her eyes searched his face. Of the sons Mary de Bohun had borne John of Bedford had always struck Joanna as the most acute and ambitious, but she had prided herself on having a good relationship with him.

'His Grace has gone again into France and I am named Regent until his return,' he said now. 'But he signed this warrant before he sailed.'

There was a document on the desk. He stabbed it with a jewelled finger.

'On what grounds? What on earth am I supposed to have done?'

'Plotted and attempted the death of the King,' he informed her.

'Plotted and att — ? In the name of God, how? For what reason?'

'Through diverse enchantments and

spells,' he answered.

'Enchantments and spells!' It was as if she were under a spell herself and could only repeat his words.

'It is already proved, Madam.'

'Proved by whom? How can a falsehood be proved?'

'No falsehood, Madam,' he said, unyielding. 'Your confessor, John Randolf, has laid information against you.'

'I demand to see him, face to face!'

'That's not possible, Madam,' he said smoothly. 'In the midst of giving his evidence, Father Randolf was overcome by temper and expired.'

'And *that*'s not possible!' she retorted. 'There was never such a mild cleric as John Randolf. I never knew him to lose his temper!'

'On this occasion,' said Bedford, 'he did.'

'And *died* of it?' Joanna choked back an hysterical giggle, another thought striking her. 'Where are my pages? Roger and Petronel?'

'They have been arrested and will be interrogated.'

'They're young lads and will say anything if they are bullied enough! And this warrant — you tell me the King signed it before he sailed to France? How comes it that the evidence is only now being collected?'

'You admit there is evidence?'

'I admit nothing!' she exclaimed angrily. 'So don't twist my words into false meaning. I have never sought to harm Henry — anybody, by any means! What's that?'

Her ears had caught a distant smashing sound, steel against oak, the splintering of wood.

'They are breaking down a locked door, I imagine,' he said shrugging.

The key at her waist weighed her down. In her mind the room appeared, with the bowls and jars, the books of spells, the crystal.

'I have harmed nobody,' she said again, and licked lips gone suddenly dry. 'At the trial — '

272

'There will be no trial, Madam.'

'No trial. I am to be condemned unheard, on a warrant signed before any evidence was taken? That is not justice!'

'It is expediency, Madam,' Bedford said.

'I did not hate Richard,' Henry had told her, 'but it was expedient for him to die.'

Richard had stood between Henry and the throne. Now she stood between Henry's son and his final conquest of France.

'It is because I would not lend him the money,' she said numbly. 'He wants Katharine as he once wanted Isabella. It is because I would not lend him the money.'

'You are to be taken to Pevensey Castle.' Bedford ignored her last remarks, though she fancied he looked a shade uncomfortable.

'Where's that?'

'On the south coast. Sir John Pelham is its custodian. You may have two of your women with you and a physician will be available.'

'I will appeal!' Her voice shrilled. 'I have sons . . . friends.'

But she knew even as she spoke that her sons would do no more than raise a few feeble protests, and she had never made any close friends.

'There is no appeal when there has been no trial,' Bedford said.

'My possessions — '

'Are forfeit to the state, Madam.'

'Rich pickings for Mary de Bohun's sons,' she said bitterly, and felt a dull pleasure as he winced. 'I was a good wife to your father and a kindly stepmother to you.'

'Sorcery is punishable by death.' He had regained his poise. 'The King, having affection for you, commutes the sentence.'

It was so clear to her now and there was nothing she could do.

'So he commits me to gaol, where no doubt I shall be murdered.'

'No Madam!' He looked genuinely

shocked. 'My royal brother intends no harm to your person!'

That was probably true, she thought wryly. Richard had had to die because he had occupied a throne. All she had could be confiscated from her without resorting to murder, though it would probably suit Henry very well if she obligingly died while she was in custody. Meanwhile the fascinating Katharine would marry him and enjoy what was really Joanna's.

'But I will outlive!' Joanna thought. The resolve, springing deep from within, stiffened her spine and dried her tears in her eyes. 'I will outlive Katharine de Valois and Henry, too, even if I have to resort to sorcery to do it.'

13

She had begun to lose count of time. Only the changing sky beyond the barred window heralded each season as it came and went. She was allowed no candles so in the winter the days began late and ended early, when she huddled beneath the coarse blankets on her straw pallet and tried not to remember the feather bolsters, the satin quilts and the lambswool covers at Langley and Havering Bower. Twice a day the two women assigned to her brought a tray of plain but adequate fare. Every morning she was escorted to the long cellar that stretched beneath the castle of Pevensey to exercise for an hour. Up and down, up and down, past rusting suits of armour and casks of wine, air blowing through the slits in the tops of the walls. Once a week she was escorted to the chapel to hear Mass, her face veiled from the inquisitive stares of those employed at the castle, her habit of grey sackcloth shrouding her frame. On rare occasions Sir John Pelham, the governor, visited the small room, bare save for the pallet and a bucket, where she spent her time. Standing near the door as if, Joanna thought ironically, he feared she might spring at him, he would give her such items of news as he considered she ought to know. The King had married Katharine de Valois, thereby ensuring the French succession to any heirs he might beget upon her, and to hammer the point home he had remained for several months in France to complete his conquests. The King had brought his French wife to London and the crowds had flocked to greet her.

'Is she beautiful?' she had not been able to resist asking.

'They say she is very lovely, Madam,' Sir John said, 'and most richly dressed, though I myself have not seen her.'

'So all my money has not been

spent on arms,' Joanna thought, but she made no comment.

Months later Sir John came to tell her of the death of Clarence and of the renewed campaign in France.

'The King has sworn to avenge his brother,' he said. 'He was slain by a Scotsman fighting with the Dauphin's troops, so now every Scot taken in battle will be hanged.'

Joanna shivered. Once she would have wept for Clarence whom she had always liked for his amiable temper and sense of fun, but even he had not raised a finger to help when Henry had sent her here.

The summer and the autumn had passed without news and then, at the beginning of December, she had received another visit from the governor.

'Queen Katharine has borne a son who will be named for his father,' Sir John said.

'I trust the babe is well,' Joanna said, but in truth she cared little either way. Henry, it was clear, had obtained his wish and Katharine had done her duty.

'Very well,' Sir John said, adding unexpectedly, 'but the King is somewhat discomposed.'

'Why?' Joanna roused briefly from her indifference.

'His Grace wished the child to be born at Westminster, that palace being under auspicious stars at the period of the confinement, but the Queen insisted on removing to Windsor a few weeks before the child was born, and Windsor is not a fortunate birthplace for this babe — or so rumour has it,' he finished somewhat lamely.

'Then Katharine defied the King.' Joanna could not repress the faint smile that rose to her lips. Little as she cared for any mention of the Valois queen, it was gratifying to be told that Henry didn't always have things his own way.

Sir John went away soon afterwards, leaving her to the cold solitude of her room again. All over England, Joanna thought, people would be rejoicing at the birth of an heir to the victor of Agincourt. Nobody would remember that the Queen Dowager had no part in the festivities.

'I brought no heir to England,' Joanna said bitterly to the empty room. 'I brought only wealth for the King to steal.'

He had evidently forgiven Katharine for her disobedience. One of her women, coming in with a tray of food, whispered as she bent to set it down,

'The Queen has sailed to France to join His Grace. They say the fighting there is worse than ever though.'

The French evidently did not have the sense to know when they were beaten.

'And neither,' Joanna thought, 'do I. By now I ought to be dead or out of my mind, but my health is good and my mind clearer than I could have hoped.'

The years in Pevensey ran into a

blur, each hour the same dun colour, but her youth was as clear as if she had lived it the day before. Herself as a child eager for her father's approval though it was rarely won. Herself as a girl at the French Court where King Charles and Queen Isabeau, the one sane and the other loving, had treated her so kindly. Herself in the pleasaunce garden where — better not to remember that! Sir Oliver Clisson had been dead for several years and she no longer permitted herself to remember his face.

Another summer with the patch of blue beyond the window streaked with autumn cloud and overhead the rays of a valiant sun.

The bolts on the outside of her door were drawn back and a cloaked figure, head held proudly above a collar thick with rubies, came in. For a moment Joanna stared, then the visitor bowed and came to embrace her.

'Humphrey! I did not recognise you,' Joanna said blankly.

'In a moment you will be telling me that I have grown,' the Duke of Gloucester said.

'More handsome.' She spoke quickly, regarding her stepson with a more cautious eye. This youngest of Henry's brothers had always been the quietest, but she had sensed a cool intelligence behind the dark eyes. He had never been particularly friendly towards her and she wondered why he should come now to greet her with such affection.

'You look well,' he said, his hands still on her shoulders as he stepped back to look at her.

'Considering I have been locked away for — how long has it been?'

'Three years, Your Grace. Too long in my opinion.'

'In mine too,' she said wryly.

'There was nothing one could do.' He released her, spreading his hand wide. 'The two boys confessed to having aided you in sorceries against the life of the King.'

'And were hanged, I suppose?' She

tried to speak lightly but her lower lip trembled, Roger and Petronel had been so young and so innocent. 'As I am myself,' she said, continuing her thought aloud.

'Are what, Your Grace?'

'Innocent!' she said sharply. 'I was under the impression that before a verdict there must be a trial and before the trial a public accusation. The meanest serf in England gets that, but the anointed Queen does not!'

'The King has released you, Madam,' Gloucester broke in. 'I persuaded him to it when I was with him in France.'

'Released?' The information was too weighty to sink into her mind. 'He has absolved me from blame?'

'You are pardoned and restored to full honours and liberty.'

'Pardoned?' She felt a sudden wild desire to laugh. 'Did they pardon Roger and Petronel too? And what of Father Randolf who they told me laid evidence against me in the first place?'

'Father Randolf died,' Gloucester said.

'Did he? How convenient.' She drew a deep breath and said, 'So it is to you I owe this? Or does my stepson's conscience begin to stir and prick?'

'Henry is dying,' Gloucester said.

'Dying! But he is not yet six and thirty! He has been wounded?'

'He had dysentery,' Gloucester said. 'It runs rife through the army. He has had several attacks and never given in to them, never admitted that he was ill, but they have weakened his constitution beyond repair. He can no longer sit his horse.'

'Henry dying.' She turned the words over in her mind, and was surprised to find regret, not for the King who had confiscated her wealth and condemned her without trial, but for the wild Prince Hal whom she had shielded on more than one occasion from his father's wrath. 'I am sorry to hear it, but glad that he sees fit to make some kind of reparation.'

'You may reside either at Langley, Leeds Castle or Havering Bower — or move between the three of them,' he told her. 'Those castles are restored to you.'

'What of my other moneys? My rents from Brittany?'

'For those it will be necessary for Your Grace to petition Parliament. You must understand that loans were raised on them to carry on the wars in France.'

'And now, having triumphed, Henry is dying.' She shook her head at the irony of it. 'Is he in England?'

'He's at Vincennes in France.'

'I know of it. The family used to go hunting there.'

'The Queen is with him. Prince Henry is at Windsor still. He's a pretty babe.'

'And will soon be King. A babe in arms to rule England?'

'The child has uncles.'

'Aye, John and yourself.' She gave him a long look and spoke softly. 'The last boy King had uncles too. He was Richard the Second.'

'I'll not make a Richard out of him,' Gloucester said.

'I? Surely you and Bedford will share the regency?'

'John is ambitious,' he said moodily. 'It will irk him to share power.'

'You too, I think?' She gave him another long look. 'And why is it you persuaded Henry to release me?'

'You have certain skills.' His glance slid away from her. 'You and I have always been good friends.'

'I always believed Henry and I were good friends,' she said, 'but it seems I was mistaken.'

'Believe me, but he bears you no grudge,' Gloucester said earnestly. 'It is his desire to be reconciled with you, with all men. He knows he will never again see England.'

Joanna, hearing the first part of his speech, opened her mouth furiously to protest that Henry had no reason to bear a grudge since she had never sought to harm him. She closed it again, aware of the implication behind her stepson's words. Gloucester actually believed that she had used sorcery against the King. His motive for helping her was clear now. He hoped she would use her arts in the power-struggle he anticipated between his brother and himself when Henry was dead. She could continue to insist upon her innocence and risk spending the rest of her life in this dismal confinement, or she could cease pleading the truth and be free.

'I am grateful for your speaking on my behalf,' she said at last. 'I hope we will continue to be good friends, Humphrey. How soon may I leave this place?'

'As soon as you please. Today if you like. I took the liberty of bringing half a dozen gowns with me, so you may choose whichever you want. Sir John Pelham has set aside a chamber where you can change.'

'I can scarcely believe it.' She spoke

dully, feeling a strange unreality cloud her feelings. The taste of freedom was too unfamiliar as yet. She was not certain what she would find to do with it.

'Come.' Gloucester held open the door with a slightly theatrical flourish.

The chamber into which she was shown had a large mirror. She caught a swift glance of a haggard, grey-clad figure and turned away abruptly, shuddering, from the stranger she had become. There were kirtles and head-dresses laid across the bed and she went to examine them, fingers sliding for the first time in three years over silk and velvet. The tub in a corner of the room was full of hot, scented water, and there were fleecy towels. She savoured the moment but not until her women had clasped the travelling-cape of grey squirrel round her shoulders did she look again in the mirror.

She had kept her figure, had even lost a little weight which suited her, but her complexion was dull and her hair, plaited beneath her hood of black velvet, was almost completely grey. It was no longer possible to think of herself as a young woman, though she flattered herself that she carried her years with dignity.

'Your Grace.' Sir John Pelham tapped on the door. 'Milord of Gloucester wishes to know if you are ready to travel.'

'Quite ready.' She dismissed the women with a nod and held out her hand to the governor. 'I cannot pretend to have enjoyed your hospitality, but I hope we meet again under happier circumstances.'

'I beg you to remember that I was only doing my duty,' he said, avoiding her hand and bowing instead. 'You will not hold it against me?'

So he, too, believed her guilty of sorcery? She restrained a bitter smile and said, 'I shall remember that you treated me with very great kindness, Sir John.'

A litter had been provided, curtained

and cushioned. Several bystanders were gathered in the courtyard. She smiled in their direction and noticed that one or two held their fingers crossed against the evil eye. They had come to take a look at the woman who, had she not been a queen, would have been drowned or hanged three years before. Joanna the witch, she reflected, and accepted Gloucester's helping hand up into the litter.

It was odd to be free again. She leaned back, closing her eyes against the too-bright light and the space beyond the litter. Two much sudden space after the bare little room. It would take her some time to become accustomed to it again.

'I thought Your Grace would like to go to Leeds Castle for a few days.' Gloucester leaned from his horse to speak to her.

'That was thoughtful of you.' She smiled her thanks, but was glad when he let the curtain drop and rode on, leaving her in peace.

Five weeks later she woke to hear the bells tolling for the death of the King. 'The King is dead! Long live the King!' She muttered the words, hoisting herself higher on her satin pillows. And the new king was an eight-month-old baby with two ambitious uncles who would fight for power. Well, they were welcome to power. She herself wanted only to be left in peace. Already she had started to make an inventory of her possessions and had petitioned Parliament for the restoration of her rents.

Later that day, dressed in black as a token of mourning, she sat at the desk in her private chamber and read Gloucester's letter, sent to her from France a few days ago.

'Henry has received Extreme Unction in a very contrite and forgiving spirit. The Queen, poor soul, is deeply distressed. She is not yet one and twenty and is already a widow. Henry had requested her to make her home in England where she can be near the babe, but Bedford and I are agreed that the child should be reared in a separate establishment. Richard was left too much with his mother and the Lady of Kent spoiled the child. This babe must be trained from the start to be a great warrior and a strong king.'

'Poor babe,' Joanna muttered, running her eye down the closely written page. Yet perhaps it was as well. She herself had been a most loving mother and stepmother, but all her children had disappointed her, save those who had died.

'I will wait here until the end comes, and then make haste to England that the funeral obsequies may be swiftly arranged. The whole nation will be in mourning for a king who brought honour and glory to the meanest of his soldiers, and I shall mourn the best of brothers.'

'Which will not prevent you from seizing power as quickly as you can,' Joanna said aloud. The habit of talking to herself had grown on her in prison and was difficult to break. She shook her head and returned to the letter.

'I am taking the liberty of sending you a new waiting woman. Her name is Eleanor Cobham and she was formerly in my wife's employ, but wishes now to change her situation.'

Meaning that Gloucester, not altogether trusting the friendship between Joanna and himself, was going to plant a spy in her household. Eleanor Cobham was probably his mistress. She put the letter back into the desk and rose, yawning, the long day stretching before her. She would have to write letters of condolence to the Queen and to Bedford and Gloucester, she supposed. Polite letters, full of regret that was not entirely hypocritical. There had been a time, before he needed money for his campaign in France, when Henry had been genuinely fond of her.

But, for the moment, the letters could wait. She went down the stone passage into the garden, rimed now with the first frosts of autumn. The apple trees were already bare, waving black branches against the wintry sky. The grass was littered with windfalls. She scooped some up, discarding those too badly bruised. Apples stewed soft and mixed with vinegar were good for sore throats.

'And let them dare to make sorcery out of that,' she muttered.

The tolling of the bells echoed still from the village church. They tolled for more than the death of a king. They tolled too for a girl in a garden, and an elderly man who talked of far-off battles, and another whose face she did not permit herself to remember. She could feel tears pricking her eyes but that was foolish, for witches cannot weep.

Epilogue

1437

There were days now when she grew a little muddled in her mind, days when she sometimes forgot the name of the attendant who was waiting upon her or sometimes believed herself to be in a different place. On this morning however she was free from headache and very clear in the brain.

She was sixty-eight years old and her step-grandson, King Henry the Sixth, was coming to visit her. That in itself was unusual since Henry was usually closeted with his tutors and seldom visited anybody. Not, she reflected, that she had gone far afield herself in the past fifteen years. With the accession of an eight-month-old child and the government of the realm in the hands of the King's uncles her own usefulness seemed to have ended. She had retired to Havering Bower and prudently kept aloof from the intrigues that swirled about the head of the frail child born to the Valois bride.

And now Katharine herself was dead, less than six months previously.

'I outlived her,' Joanna muttered.

'Your Grace?' One of her ladies looked at her questioningly.

'I wish to read over my Will again,' she said in a louder tone.

'Madam, you had the clerks bring it yesterday.'

'Did I? Well, there is probably no time before the King comes anyway. Is my headdress straight?'

'Yes, Your Grace. You look beautiful.'

'You're a great liar, Agnes,' Joanna remarked without emotion. 'Oh, when I was a girl I was lovely then, but I'm dried up now, a painted stick of a thing to be shied at at a tawdry fair.'

'Your Grace has put on a little weight,' Agnes admitted.

'A fat painted stick,' Joanna said.

She was in an excellent humour. This was one of the days when the past seemed to be bathed in a rosy glow. She had once been lovely. She had known two contented marriages. Even her surviving children were improving, though Richard was in failing health and had never been very energetic even when he was well. Jean-Pierre had settled into a comfortable middle age as had Marie, and Arthur, released from his captivity ten years before, was winning a name for himself as one of the most valiant knights in Europe. Best of all she need never worry about being poor again. In his Will the late King had restored to her all her rents and revenues and, in the years since, she had invested wisely.

At Havering Bower the trees were heavy with ripening fruit, the deer-park well stocked, the ponds leaping with carp. Within fires blazed in every apartment for she felt cold even in summer, and cargoes of silk and ivory carried by her trading ships decorated each chamber.

'Do you think,' she enquired now, 'that Henry will bring me a present?'

'Madam, he is certain to do so — and you have one for him yourself.'

'Aye, a pot of green ginger,' Joanna nodded, adding somewhat hastily, 'Lads are fond of spicy food.'

'Indeed, Your Grace.'

A pleasant girl, Agnes, but a fool, forever bobbing into curtsies and agreeing with one. She did not, however, moan for an increase in wages as did some of the other servants and, for that reason alone, Joanna was disposed to favour her.

'The King is coming.' The page stationed at the window turned to announce the fact.

Joanna reached for her ivory-headed cane and rose. Beyond the window she could hear the clatter of hoofs and harness, and a moment later the young King, flanked by his cousin of Warwick and Milord Gloucester, entered.

She had not seen him for some years and he had grown so much that she found herself looking up at him. He was not yet in proportion, his neck and wrists too long and thin, his fair hair still retaining its baby curl. There was a tinge of red in it revealed by a ray of sunlight which struck through the window and haloed his head. He was not much like his father, she considered, but there was something familiar in his face. She could not put her finger exactly on what it was.

'Please to sit, Madam Grandmother.' He had a boy's voice, hovering between treble and bass. 'We are to be informal, are we not?'

'If such is Your Grace's will. I must confess I am somewhat troubled by the ague,' she confessed.

'I will make a novena to St Vitus for you,' the boy said. 'He cures many afflicted with the shivering and trembling.'

'Thank you.' She bowed her head, thinking that the remedies she concocted herself would probably be more effective, but it would not do to say so since the lad was evidently pious.

'You know my lords,' Henry said.

'Indeed I do.' Glancing at her stepsons, she was reminded of two hawks hovering over a dove. They shared government of the King's person between them and were always at his elbow, one not trusting the other. Like hawks, she repeated to herself.

'You look splendid, Madam!' Warwick said heartily.

'I keep in excellent health, save for pains in my head,' she returned.

'Do you get headaches?' Henry said, with the concern in his face that seemed to be habitual with him. 'I also get them from time to time, usually when I fast or have been studying for a long time.'

He looked as if he spent too many hours at his books. There were already shadows beneath his eyes and an inkstain on his forefinger.

'His Grace will be known as the

scholar prince,' said his uncle of Gloucester proudly.

'I would liefer be a good man,' Henry said. 'It is not scholarship that wins Heaven but good deeds.'

The boy was growing into a prig, Joanna decided. There had been priggishness in his father but at this lad's age he had been on campaign in the Welsh mountains, not prating morality. She moved to a seat closer to the fire and motioned him to take a chair near to her. A servant entered with wine and comfits and the two dukes relaxed slightly, taking up their position at a little distance.

'I have a gift for you,' Joanna told the boy. 'A pot of green ginger prepared by myself.'

She ignored Warwick's lifted eyebrow.

Henry gave her his singularly charming smile which irradiated his somewhat plain features.

'I am very fond of green ginger,' he said, 'but this is your birthday, so it is for me to give you a present.'

'I expected nothing beyond the honour of your visit,' she said, and saw Warwick's eyebrow fly heavenward again.

'It is a tablet of ivory.' The King beckoned a servant who approached with it. 'You may rest a book on it. The frame is of gold and the page-marker is set with a diamond.'

'Very beautiful and very ingenious!' She spoke with genuine pleasure, her eye quickly assessing its value.

'Reading is a great pleasure to me,' he said simply.

It was the remark of a lonely boy brought up in solitude without friends.

'What else do you like to do?' she enquired.

'I like fishing.' He hesitated slightly, glancing towards his uncles. 'Also riding, if the horse be not too spirited. And listening to sermons gives the mind much food for thought.'

They were rearing him to be a monk and not a King, she thought. In that manner they could keep the power longer in their own hands. The uncles of Richard the Second had followed the same course with lamentable results.

She was relieved when Henry, gazing thoughtfully at a couple of her younger attendants withdrawn to a polite distance near the door, confided,

'I am fond also of the conversation of young ladies. I have portraits of all the princesses in Europe and I hope to be married with one of them one day. I will take the prettiest.'

'But you have not chosen yet?'

'When my education is completed and I begin to rule.' He had blushed a little. 'I would like to found schools where more boys could learn to read and write.'

'His Grace's heart is in the right place,' Gloucester said.

'But my uncle does not believe my head is,' the boy said with a disconcerting flash of shrewdness. 'He does not believe that the first duty of a king is to relieve the ignorance and distress of his subjects.'

'Your father was a great warrior,' Gloucester said.

'But in the end we had to make treaty with my cousin of France,' Henry returned. 'So many lives lost and so much money wasted on fruitless campaigns.'

The boy had a will of his own after all, Joanna thought. It was clear however that he would find no chance of exercising it while her stepsons held the reins. Already they were beginning to rise, signalling the visit was at an end.

'It has been so good to see you again,' Henry said, with such fervour in his voice that she felt a pang of pity. The lad must lead a dull existence if a duty visit to an old woman afforded him such pleasure.

'I hope you will come again.' She began to stoop to kiss his hand, but he embraced her instead, his beardless cheek warm against her painted one.

'I will enjoy the green ginger,' he said, 'for you prepared it with your

own hands which shows true affection.
I will eat a little every day when I have
made my devotions and as I eat I will
send up a prayer for your good health,
which will be a bond between us.'

He smiled again that smile of
extraordinary sweetness and she knew
on the instant of whom he had
reminded her. She was transported
back more than fifty years to herself as a
girl, bidding farewell to the Valois King
and his Queen. Charles de Valois, of
crazy memory, with the sweetly vacant
smile and the restless hands forever
plucking at his garments as this boy's
hands were plucking now. There was
scarcely anything in him of his father
or of Katharine, but of his grandfather
there was already too much.

Gloucester lingered as the others
went out, pitching his voice low.

'We are not as we seem,' he said.

Not hawks but guardians, watching
over a precious charge, fearing the taint
of Valois blood.

'If my arts could help,' she answered

low, 'I would offer them, but they cannot.'

'He is an innocent.' He spoke heavily. 'Our only hope is to guard the knowledge of it from himself and others for as long as we can, and marry him to some strong-minded girl whose wit will supply his want.'

'I will pray for your success,' she began.

'To which god?' he returned and was gone before she could frame a reply.

'Such a charming boy!' Agnes had darted to the window. 'They are saying he will be a saintly king when he comes into his own.'

But he never will, Joanna thought with a piercing clarity that, for a moment, stripped the veils of age from her mind. My sun is setting, but his will never truly rise. The revenge I sought when Henry imprisoned me so that he could marry the Valois princess is blossoming.

It was a bitter harvest in which she took no pleasure.

Then the moment passed as the pounding at her temples began. She picked up the tablet of ivory and gold, silently fighting the pain as she calculated its monetary value. The girl in the garden would die wealthy and that was all that mattered to her now.

Other titles in the Linford Romance Library

SAVAGE PARADISE
Sheila Belshaw ✓

For four years, Diana Hamilton had dreamed of returning to Luangwa Valley in Zambia. Now she was back — and, after a close encounter with a rhino — was receiving a lecture from a tall, khaki-clad man on the dangers of going into the bush alone!

PAST BETRAYALS
Giulia Gray ✓

As soon as Jon realized that Julia had fallen in love with him, he broke off their relationship and returned to work in the Middle East. When Jon's best friend, Danny, proposed a marriage of friendship, Julia accepted. Then Jon returned and Julia discovered her love for him remained unchanged.

PRETTY MAIDS ALL IN A ROW
Rose Meadows

The six beautiful daughters of George III of England dreamt of handsome princes coming to claim them, but the King always found some excuse to reject proposals of marriage. This is the story of what befell the Princesses as they began to seek lovers at their father's court, leaving behind rumours of secret marriages and illegitimate children.

THE GOLDEN GIRL
Paula Lindsay

Sarah had everything — wealth, social background, great beauty and magnetic charm. Her heart was ruled by love and compassion for the less fortunate in life. Yet, when one man's happiness was at stake, she failed him — and herself.

A DREAM OF HER OWN
Barbara Best

A stranger gently kisses Sarah Danbury at her Betrothal Ball. Little does she realise that she is to meet this mysterious man again in very different circumstances.

HOSTAGE OF LOVE
Nara Lake

From the moment pretty Emma Tregear, the only child of a Van Diemen's Land magnate, met Philip Despard, she was desperately in love. Unfortunately, handsome Philip was a convict on parole.

THE ROAD TO BENDOUR
Joyce Eaglestone

Mary Mackenzie had lived a sheltered life on the family farm in Scotland. When she took a job in the city she was soon in a romantic maze from which only she could find the way out.

NEW BEGINNINGS
Ann Jennings

On the plane to his new job in a hospital in Turkey, Felix asked Harriet to put their engagement on hold, as Philippe Krir, the Director of Bodrum hospital, refused to hire 'attached' people. But, without an engagement ring, what possible excuse did Harriet have for holding Philippe at bay?

THE CAPTAIN'S LADY
Rachelle Edwards

1820: When Lianne Vernon becomes governess at Elswick Manor, she finds her young pupil is given to strange imaginings and that her employer, Captain Gideon Lang, is the most enigmatic man she has ever encountered. Soon Lianne begins to fear for her pupil's safety.

THE VAUGHAN PRIDE
Margaret Miles

As the new owner of Southwood Manor, Laura Vaughan discovers that she's even more poverty stricken than before. She also finds that her neighbour, the handsome Marius Kerr, is a little too close for comfort.

HONEY-POT
Mira Stables

Lovely, well-born, well-dowered, Russet Ingram drew all men to her. Yet here she was, a prisoner of the one man immune to her graces — accused of frivolously tampering with his young ward's romance!

DREAM OF LOVE
Helen McCabe

When there is a break-in at the art gallery she runs, Jade can't believe that Corin Bossinney is a trickster, or that she'd fallen for the oldest trick in the book . . .

FOR LOVE OF OLIVER
Diney Delancey ♡

When Oliver Scott buys her family home, Carly retains the stable block from which she runs her riding school. But she soon discovers Oliver is not an easy neighbour to have. Then Carly is presented with a new challenge, one she must face for love of Oliver.

THE SECRET OF MONKS' HOUSE
Rachelle Edwards ♡

Soon after her arrival at Monks' House, Lilith had been told that it was haunted by a monk, and she had laughed. Of greater interest was their neighbour, the mysterious Fabian Delamaye. Was he truly as debauched as rumour told, and what was the truth about his wife's death?

THE SPANISH HOUSE
Nancy John

Lynn couldn't help falling in love with the arrogant Brett Sackville. But Brett refused to believe that she felt nothing for his half-brother, Rafael. Lynn knew that the cruel game Brett made her play to protect Rafael's heart could end only by breaking hers.

PROUD SURGEON
Lynne Collins

Calder Savage, the new Senior Surgical Officer at St. Antony's Hospital, had really lived up to his name, venting a savage irony on anyone who fell foul of him. But when he gave Staff Nurse Honor Portland a lift home, she was surprised to find what an interesting man he was.